Mountain of Deception

by

Carol Preflatish

Romantic Suspense from
Dragonfly Publishing, Inc.

MOUNTAIN OF DECEPTION

Romantic Suspense

Paperback Edition
EAN 978-1-941278-24-6
ISBN 1-941278-24-8

Published in the United States of America by
Dragonfly Publishing, Inc.
www.dragonflypubs.com

* * * * *

CHAPTER 1

TESSA Cooper drove through the small town of Yellowwood, Tennessee just outside Smoky Mountains National Park.

The highway ran down what she would call the tourist strip, although, from what she had researched online, not many tourists had discovered Yellowwood yet. Most of them opted for Gatlinburg or Pigeon Forge with their many attractions, shops, and hotels.

Her GPS instructed her to turn right at the next road to find the cabin she would be renting for the next twelve months. After the turn, she drove up a long hill before it leveled off where she found the cabin. A car in the driveway with a sign on the side identified its owner, the real estate agent she had been talking with for the past few weeks.

Tessa parked her car and stepped out. An older lady with bright red hair approached. "Tessa Cooper?"

"Yes."

"Oh good. I'm glad you found the cabin. Honey, I'm Claire Borden. We've been talkin' on the phone." Her southern accent was prominent.

"It's nice to meet you, Mrs. Borden."

"Oh, sweetie, we aren't all that fancy around here. You call me Claire."

"Claire it is, and I'm Tessa."

"Come on in. I'll show you around. I know you're going to love it."

Tessa looked around as she and Claire walked to the house. She could already tell she was going to love living here. The view of the mountains behind the cabin was spectacular. There was another cabin across the road, and she thought she had seen another up the road when she turned into the driveway.

Once inside, Claire showed her all the rooms, and Tessa loved the inside as much as the outside. "Mrs. Borden, the cabin is beautiful. It will be perfect for me to stay in to write my novel," Tessa said.

"Now call me Claire, remember?"

"I'm sorry. Claire."

"I knew you would like it. I have all the paperwork with me and you can move your things in right now." She dug a folder of papers out of her bag, and they sat down at the kitchen table.

Tessa took her time to carefully look over the lease and then signed two copies. "I think that should do it."

Claire signed both copies as well and then gave Tessa one of them. "All utilities are included in the rent, but you'll probably want to buy some wood for the fireplace on those really cold winter nights, or," her lips curled into a smile, "when you have a gentleman caller."

Tessa laughed. "I think I'll just stick to a fire to keep me warm."

"Well, we'll see. Here's my card. Now, if you have any problems, you be sure and call me, you hear? The owners are livin' in Florida now, and I take care of everything for them."

"Thank you." Tessa followed Claire outside.

Just then, a large black pickup truck turned into the gravel driveway and parked next to Tessa's car. The door opened and out stepped a rugged-looking man dressed in a tight T-shirt and jeans. His mane of long brown hair framed the surly expression on his face. A folded handkerchief over his forehead held his hair out of his face. He held a tool belt in his left hand and lifted a big toolbox from the truck bed with his right. His upper arm muscles bulged, and Tessa thought for sure his shirt would rip *Hulk* style.

"Silas, darlin', come on over here. I want you to meet the new renter." Claire motioned for him to join them. "Silas Newberry, this is Tessa Cooper. She'll be livin' here for the next twelve months while she writes a novel."

Silas wiped his hand on his jeans and looked up at Tessa as he extended his hand. Her gaze traced from his hand and up his arm until their eyes met. The surly expression gone, a smile spread across his dark, tanned face. His blue eyes sparkled.

"Twelve months?" he questioned.

"I'm on a sabbatical from teaching."

"Well, how do you do, ma'am. Welcome to Yellowwood." His voice was deep, but soft with just a tad bit of southern drawl.

She shook his hand, finding it rough. Normal for a man carrying tools, she thought. "Thank you. It's nice to meet you," she replied, probably holding his hand a bit too long. He withdrew first.

"Tessa, Silas is our local handyman. He can build or fix just about anything. He'll probably be around a lot since he's buildin' a storage building out back for the cabin owners," Claire said.

"Oh, a storage building, that's nice."

"I hope my hammering won't interrupt your writing, ma'am."

"No, I'm sure it won't."

How in the world was she going to get any writing done with this handsome man hanging around everyday?

"Well, I better get to work. It was nice meeting you, Miss Cooper."

"Tessa. You might as well call me Tessa since you'll be around a lot."

"Okay, Tessa. Mrs. Borden." He nodded to both and headed to the back of the house.

Both ladies watched him walk away. No doubt Claire was enjoying the view as much as Tessa.

"Oh my." Claire took a deep breath, and Tessa thought she actually heard her swoon. "He's such a nice young man and single too."

Tessa realized that Claire was hinting about Silas. "I didn't come here to find another husband, just to write a book."

"Oh, you've been married before?"

"I'm a widow. My husband passed away a few years ago from an illness."

"I'm sorry to hear that, dear. You're so young to be a widow," Claire said.

"Thank you."

"Well, I should be goin'. Now, don't you neglect to call me if you need anythin'."

"Thank you. I appreciate you helping me."

The sound of hammering echoed though the air from the back yard. "The view from the kitchen window is the best." Claire winked and then got into her car and drove away.

Tessa unloaded her car and took everything into the house. Then, she took a drive into town to get her mail delivery set up. Her best friend, Sara, had promised to ship her the things that wouldn't fit into the car. She also picked up a few necessities at the grocery store and was shocked at the high price of food. It was well into the evening by the time she had everything put away and settled in.

Tessa slept later than normal the following day. She attributed it to being so tired from her long drive the day before. Once she was up, she went to the kitchen and started a pot of coffee. While it brewed, she jumped into the shower. Mentally, she planned her day. Breakfast. Writing. Lunch. And more writing. Heck, at that pace, she'd have her book finished in no time.

She stepped out of the shower, dried off, and dressed. When she opened the bathroom door, she could smell the aroma of the coffee.

In the kitchen, she got a bagel, sliced it, and put it in the toaster. After pouring herself a cup of coffee, she turned and saw a man walk by the kitchen window. Startled, she nearly dropped her cup, but then felt a little silly when she realized it was Silas coming to work on the shed.

The bagel popped up from the toaster, and she got the cream cheese from the refrigerator. With everything on the table, she positioned herself where she could watch Silas work while she ate breakfast.

Mmm-hmm. This was what Mrs. Borden had meant about the view from the kitchen window. "What a way to start a morning."

Each day afterward for the next week, she sat at the same place so she could watch Silas work while eating her breakfast and lunch. He certainly was easy on the eyes, and she enjoyed watching him work up a sweat. Some days he would wear his hair loose with the handkerchief around his forehead like the day they met. Other days he would pull it back into a small ponytail. Each day, she tried to work up the courage to ask him in for lunch. But it had been so long since she had any interest in a man, she felt pretty rusty with how to do it and always chickened out.

If she were still in Illinois, she would start the morning with a workout at the physical education building at the university. Instead, she hadn't done anything but eat and sit at the computer. She could already tell it was having an impact on her. She decided to start the day with a brisk walk outside. The morning was cool, but she knew that even in the mountains the August heat would build as the day wore on.

She had been walking along the road for about fifteen minutes when she saw Silas approaching in his truck.

"Good morning. Getting your exercise in?" He leaned against the open window as he came to a stop.

"I like to get the adrenaline going in the morning. It helps me through the day."

He smiled. "I know what you mean, but I usually get mine going with a lot of coffee."

Tessa laughed. "I doubt that. You look like you work out all the time." She felt like a silly schoolgirl with a crush on the quarterback.

"There's a fitness club in town where I try to go to a few times a week to lift weights."

"That's good to know. I might have to check that out."

"You'd like it. In the meantime, make sure you keep an eye out for bears on your walks out here," he warned.

"What do you mean?"

"The bears are active mostly in the mornings, and there have been a few show up around here looking for food. Normally, they stay inside the park, but the neighbors have spotted a few in the area before. You certainly don't want to leave any food outside for them to smell. You're just asking for trouble then."

"Thanks for the warning. I'll be careful."

He smiled and waved as he put his truck in gear and drove off. She looked around both sides of the road for signs of bears, not that she would know what a sign would be. Thick brush and trees lined the road, and it occurred to her that maybe she should hurry back to the cabin and look up the number for that fitness center. She started back up the hill at a much brisker gait than she had when she walked down.

When she neared her home, she spotted the lady that lived across the street from her at the mailbox. This was as good of a time as any to start meeting the neighbors. "Hello, I'm Tessa Cooper, your new neighbor."

"Hello, it's nice to meet you. I'm Elaine Pratt. I saw you moving things in the cabin, but wasn't sure if you were going to be a permanent resident or just a tourist on vacation."

"Well, I'm not really a tourist or a permanent resident. I've leased the cabin for a year, taking a sabbatical from teaching at a university up north."

"Well, welcome to the neighborhood then. You'll love it here. It's nice and quiet." Just as she said that, they heard Silas start up an electric saw. "Well, most of the time it's quiet. As long as it's attached to that handsome body, I can put up with a little noise, right?"

A man walked out of Elaine's home. "Elaine, did the newspaper come yet?" he called.

"Yes, dear. Come out and meet our new neighbor," she answered.

The older man with graying hair at his temples came out. "Hello," he said.

"Martin, this is Tessa Cooper. She's leased the cabin across the road for a year to—what did you say you were doing?"

"I didn't actually, but I'm hoping to spend my year off from work writing a novel," Tessa answered.

"Oh, how exciting. You'll have to tell me all about it," Elaine exclaimed.

Martin took the newspaper from Elaine's hand and turned to Tessa. "It was nice meeting you." He walked back to the house.

"He's not much of a conversationalist until he's had his morning coffee and read the paper."

Tessa just nodded.

"Since you're new around here, I'll have to show you where everything is in town."

"Well, I've already found the post office, supermarket, and restaurants."

"Oh honey, those are for the tourists, and they charge outrageous prices."

"You're right about that," Tessa replied. "I spent a small fortune on groceries the other day.

"What are you doing after lunch? I have to go to get groceries myself, and you can come along."

"I guess I could. I was planning on writing this afternoon, but I suppose that can wait a few hours."

"Wonderful! You be ready at one-o'clock, and I'll pick you up."

"Okay."

Elaine headed back to her home, and Tessa did the same. Since she would be out this afternoon, she decided to work on her book a little more this morning, taking her laptop and a cup of coffee to the patio table behind the cabin, which also offered her a better view of Silas working. After an hour of writing, he walked toward her.

"Working on your book?" he asked.

"A little, yes."

"What's it about?" He sat down in the other chair.

"You know, writers don't like to talk about their book until it's finished."

He laughed. "That's a polite way of saying none of your business?"

"No, no. That's not what I meant at all. I just don't like talking about it much. Not yet anyway. I can tell you it's a mystery and takes place in the mountains of Tennessee."

"I like mysteries. I'll have to make sure to get a copy when it's published."

She appreciated the fact he thought she would get it published. He took off the handkerchief around his head, letting his hair fall around his face, and wiped the sweat from his neck.

"You read?" she asked.

"Yes, I can read."

"Oh no, that's not what I meant. I just thought that most men who work in a labor type job would rather watch sports than sit and read a book." She had already put her foot in her mouth, and she was only making it worse the more she spoke.

Silas laughed. "I knew what you meant. I was teasing you."

"Oh. Would you like to come in for some lunch?" She just blurted it out and couldn't believe she just asked him that.

"You know, I did forget my lunch today and was just about to go into town to get a sandwich, but I'd hate to turn down an invitation."

"I'm afraid it'll only be a sandwich here too."

"That's fine with me. I prefer the company here, rather than the gas station in town."

"Come on inside. Does ham and cheese sound okay?"

"It sounds perfect."

He followed her inside and sat down at the kitchen table while she got the lunchmeat and cheese out of the refrigerator. "If you'd like to wash up, the bathroom is at the end of the hallway."

He got up and headed down the hall. When he returned, she had his sandwich made on a plate at the table. He'd put his handkerchief back around his head. He sat down, and she finished putting together her sandwich. Before sitting with him, she got two glasses from the cabinet and poured them each them some lemonade.

"This looks great," he said.

"Thank you. It's nice sharing lunch with someone. I miss having lunch with my friends at home."

"Where are you from?"

"Illinois. I teach English at Northeastern University up there. Are you originally from here in Yellowwood?"

"I'm from a little bit of everywhere. An English professor, wow. Teaching at a college must really be interesting."

"Yes, I do enjoy it. My husband taught history there."

Damn! Why bring him up?

"Oh, you're married, and he let you leave for a year to write?" He devoured the sandwich.

"No. He passed away a couple years ago. After that, I dived back into teaching and this is the first break I've taken since."

After another bite, he swallowed. "I'm sorry to hear about your husband, but you definitely came to the right place to get away. Just wait until the leaves turn next month. It's beautiful around here in the fall. It could be great inspiration for a writer." He finished his sandwich, and they sat in pleasant silence for a moment. "Well, I probably should be getting back to work. Thanks for the sandwich, and it was really nice talking with you." He finished his lemonade, got up, and took his plate and glass to the sink.

"I need to get going too." She put her plate and glass in the sink too. "The lady across the street is taking me into town to show me where I need to shop to avoid the tourist prices."

He looked up at her. "You've met the Pratts?"

"Yes, this morning. Why, is there something wrong with them?"

"No, not at all. They should be good neighbors. Thanks again for lunch." He turned and left.

Tessa thought his reaction to her mentioning the Pratts was a bit odd, but then she didn't know Silas well enough to read him. It had been a fun, but short lunch, and the most relaxed she'd felt all week. She made a mental note to ask him for lunch again.

Later than afternoon, Tessa rode with Elaine Pratt, who showed her around the town, including the location of the fitness center. Lastly, they stopped at the supermarket, a different one than Tessa had visited earlier. Inside, Elaine purchased her regular groceries with Tessa getting some frozen meals, more ham and cheese, and a couple bottles of wine.

When they arrived back at Tessa's house, they saw Silas' truck still in the driveway. Before Tessa got out of the car, Elaine touched her arm to stop her. "I don't know how you can get anything done with that gorgeous man working in your backyard."

"Yeah, the hammering can be distracting when I'm trying to concentrate on my writing."

"You're joking, right?"

"I try to work in the living room, so I can't see him, but if I work in the kitchen with the view of the backyard, I don't get much done."

Tessa couldn't hold her laughter in any longer and both ladies broke into hysterics.

"Martin said he was thinking of hiring him to do some work for us. I told him I was all for it."

"You didn't tell him why you were all for it, did you?" she teased as she pulled a bottled water from her bag.

"Of course not. Oh, I just had a great idea. Why don't you come to dinner at our house next Friday night, and you could bring Silas as your date."

Tessa nearly choked. "What? Date? No, I don't think that would be a good idea."

"Why not? You're interested in him, right?"

"Well, I, I don't really even know him. Besides, like I told the realtor, I'm didn't come here looking for a husband."

"Who said anything about a husband? It doesn't hurt to sniff the bread when you walk by the bakery, now does it?"

Tessa burst out laughing again. "I guess you're right. I'll think about it. I better get inside before my frozen meals thaw."

She got out and took her bags from the back seat. She lost her grip on the bag with the wine inside, and Silas seemed to appear out of nowhere to catch it. "Thanks," she said to him.

He looked inside. "This looks too valuable to break."

"Don't forget about Friday," Elaine called out the car window after Tessa had closed the door. She backed out of the driveway and drove across the street to her house.

"Let me carry these in for you." Silas took the other bag from her and followed as she unlocked the door and went inside.

He placed the bags on her counter. "You better get this stuff in the freezer before it thaws. It's really hot out today."

"Good idea." She opened the door to the freezer and put the boxes inside. "Would you like some sweet tea?"

"Actually, some cold water would be prefect."

She opened the refrigerator and got a bottle of water. "Here you go."

He unscrewed the lid and tilted the bottle up to drink. Beads of sweat ran down his face and neck finally being captured by the neckline of his T-shirt. As she continued to watch him guzzle the whole bottle in one drink, she considered the idea of them going to dinner at the Pratts' together. As he swallowed the last drop, she lost the nerve to ask him. He handed her the empty bottle. "Thanks. I better get back to work before the rain starts."

"Oh, is it supposed to rain?"

"Yeah, we're supposed to get some thundershowers later. I'm hoping to get the roof covered before it starts. Thanks again for the water."

"Thanks for carrying in my groceries." She watched as he headed out and then up the ladder to work on the roof.

* * *

THAT evening, Tessa sat on the couch and called her best friend back home in Illinois. "Hi, Sara, how's things up north?"

"Tessa, it's so good to hear from you. Things are fine up here. It's hot and humid, as usual. The air conditioning went out in our building today, and everyone got to leave early. How are things down there? How's the book writing?"

"It's hot down here too, but not as humid. The book writing is going okay. I called to talk to you about something."

"Sure, what is it?"

"Well, there's this guy down here."

"Oh my God, you met a man! That's great. Tell me all about him."

Sara had kept trying to talk her into dating again once Colin had been gone for a while, but Tessa never felt ready.

"Calm down. It's not like that. He's a carpenter, and he's building a storage building out behind my cabin."

"That is so hot. He's good-looking, right?"

Tessa hesitated just a second before answering. "Yeah, he's gorgeous," she admitted.

"So tell me more."

"He's about six foot tall, broad shoulders, very muscular, brown hair down to his shoulders, and the most gorgeous blue eyes you've ever seen."

"Sounds nice. What's the problem?"

"My neighbor across the street asked me to have dinner with her and her husband Friday night, and she wants me to bring Silas."

"His name is Silas. That's such a sexy name. So, what's the problem?"

Tessa took a sip of her chamomile tea and pulled her legs up under her. "I've only been here for two weeks. That's not really long enough to know a man before asking him to go to a dinner party with you."

"Oh, Tessa. You've been out of the dating scene for too long. Nowadays, most couples sleep together on their first date."

"That is definitely not going to happen, if we do go to dinner," she immediately replied.

"Easy girl, it's not a rule. Do you like this guy?"

"Well, yes, I think I do. He seems really nice, and he had lunch with me once this week."

"See, you've already had your first date. Do you think he likes you?"

"He seems to. He helped carry my groceries in today."

"What would it hurt to ask him? You said dinner is at the neighbors across the street, right?'

"Yes."

"Then, it's just a walk across the street, and you can come home whenever you want. I think it would be the perfect date."

"You really think so?"

"I do. It's time for you to get back out there."

Tessa grimaced. "Maybe so. I guess I could ask him tomorrow."

"Fantastic! Then, on Saturday morning you have to call me and tell me all about it and try and get a picture of him to send me. I want to see what this gorgeous man looks like."

"I'll see what I can do. Thanks, Sara. I wish you were here with me."

"Me, too. I miss our lunches together."

Tessa sat up. "Why don't you come down here for Labor Day? It's a long weekend at school. You could fly down to the airport in Knoxville, and I could pick you up."

"That sounds like fun, and I'd love to see your cabin and meet Silas."

"Let's do that then. Get your flight reservations and then let me know."

"I'll do that first thing tomorrow."

"Great. Thanks again for the talk. I better get off of here so I can figure out how I'm going to ask him."

"Keep me updated. Bye."

"I will. Bye." Tessa disconnected the call and sat quietly for a few minutes until she heard rain hitting the metal roof of the cabin. "Damn." Rain meant Silas might not be working tomorrow.

She yawned and headed to bed. While thinking of Silas, the relaxing sound of the rain falling onto the cabin's metal roof soothed her right to sleep.

When Tessa woke the next morning, she heard the rain still hitting the roof, along with thunder. That meant her invitation would probably have to wait.

At her desk in the living room, she sat down to work on her book, but her mind wandered back to the memory of Silas in her kitchen drinking that bottle of water yesterday. A knock at the kitchen door startled her out of her daydream, and hoping it was Silas, she rushed to greet him. Opening the door, she found a small-framed woman with mostly gray hair.

"Hello, dear, I'm Mae Nicholson, and I live a little up the road from here. I've come to welcome you to the neighborhood." She held up a basket and pulled back the towel to show muffins inside.

"Hello, Mrs. Nicholson. I'm Tessa Cooper. Please come in." She held the door for the older woman to enter. "Thank you for the muffins. They look wonderful."

Mae placed the basket on the kitchen table and then removed her coat and rain bonnet. Tessa took them and hung both on the hook by the door.

"Please sit down. Would you like some coffee? I just made a pot, and we could have one of your delicious looking muffins to go with it." Tessa said, having a feeling Mae wanted to stay and talk.

"That would be lovely, dear."

Tessa got two cups from the cabinet and poured the coffee, wondering what the lady wanted. "Cream or sugar?"

"Sugar is fine."

Tessa brought the coffee and sugar to the table. Then, she went back to get two small plates and some napkins before joining Mae at the table. Each of them took a muffin.

"These are delicious," Tessa said after taking a bite. "I love banana nut muffins."

"Thank you. I have a special recipe I use. You don't sound like you're from the south," Mae said, stirring sugar into her coffee, looking around the kitchen and in toward the living room.

"I'm from northern Illinois and—"

"You look like you've moved in," Mae interrupted. "Did you buy this place?"

Tessa thought, how bold of Mae to interrogate her like that, but she understood how nosey neighbors could be.

"No, I'm renting. I usually teach English at a university, but I'm taking a year off from teaching to write a novel."

"A novel, oh my. I had no idea you were a novelist. Have I read anything you've written?"

"I'm not a novelist yet. This will be my first book, if it gets published."

Mae took a sip of coffee. "What's it about?"

"It's still in its early stages, and I'm not sure where it's going yet."

"I see. Well, I best be going," Mae said abruptly and stood. Putting on her raincoat and bonnet, she added, "It was nice meeting you. I'm sure we'll see lots of each other."

"Wait, let me put these muffins in another container, and you can take your basket with you," Tessa said.

"Don't worry about that, honey. You hold onto it, and I'll pick it up another time."

Tessa stood at the door and waved goodbye to the odd little lady. She had a feeling she was going to be seeing lots of Mae Nicholson. Maybe sooner more than later.

After a few days of rain, Tessa was getting cabin fever and needed to get out of the house. Since Silas was not coming to work, it would be a good time to go into town for a workout at the fitness center.

She changed into some workout clothes and left for the center. Inside, she went to her usual treadmill, put in her ear buds, turned on her music, and started walking. Once she loosened up, she increased the pace a little. Mirrors hung on the wall above the line of treadmills, and Tessa could see the whole room. Behind her were a line of stair-step machines and behind those were spin bikes. Along the farthest wall from her was the weight-lifting equipment.

As she gazed into the mirrors, looking around the room, she spotted a familiar body. Silas sat up from the weight bench and picked up a towel to dry his face. He looked around the room and her way, and took notice. Tessa looked down at her machine, concentrating on the numbers on the display, or at least, she hoped she appeared to be looking at the numbers.

She was more worried about whether he saw her ogling him and didn't dare look up his way again.

"Mind if I join you?"

She took out her ear buds and turned, but knew who it was. "Oh, hi, Silas. Sure, be my guest."

He draped his towel over the front of the machine, stepped on the treadmill next to her, and adjusted the settings to match her pace. "How long have you been coming here?"

"This is my third visit. With it raining out, I thought it would be a good time to get a workout in. Thanks for telling me about this place. It's great here."

Silas was dressed in a tank top and shorts with his usual bandanna around his head. Tessa tried not to stare at his arm muscles, but they were so big.

He readjusted the setting to keep up with her. "You must keep in good shape, you're practically running."

She had been so nervous about him being next to her, she had increased to a rather rapid pace. She slowed herself down. "I like to do a sprint every once in a while." She matched his rhythm, and beads of perspiration ran down her back. "You don't look like a treadmill kind of guy."

"I just finished my weight-lifting when I saw you. If you're close to being finished, would you like to get something to drink at the juice bar?"

"That sounds really good, and I am finished." She stopped her machine and stepped off. Silas did the same and they both grabbed their towels. She wasn't about to miss an opportunity to spend some time with him.

After wiping down their treadmills, they walked together to the juice bar in the front of the building. Tessa took a seat at the table while Silas got them some orange juice and then joined her.

"Thanks, I can really use this," she said before taking a drink.

"Do you still like living here?"

"Oh, yes. It's so much more peaceful than living in the city. I could get used to this place."

"That's good to hear." He smiled at her.

She took another sip of her drink.

"Have you visited any of our local attractions?"

"Not really. I did stop at the Visitor's Center in town and picked up some brochures though."

"You should really try to visit some of the sights inside the park.

There's some beautiful spots in there. Maybe I could take you sometime." His smile broadened.

"That would be nice." She tried to gather the nerve to ask him about the dinner. "Silas, do you know Martin and Elaine Pratt that live across the street from me?"

"I've met them a time or two."

"Elaine asked me to dinner at their house tonight, and she mentioned that maybe you would like to come too." There, she said it. She held her breath waiting for an answer.

"Sure. It sounds like fun." His smile had reached all the way to his blue eyes. They melted her.

She was both thrilled and apprehensive upon hearing his answer. "Really? I mean, good. I'm sorry it's such short notice, but with the rain you've not been working, and I didn't know how to get in touch with you. It's casual dress, and we're expected around seven o'clock." She rambled on and couldn't stop.

"Okay, I have a couple things to do at home this afternoon, but it sounds like fun."

"Where do you live?"

"Not too far. Should I come to your house first so we can go over there together?"

"Yes, that would probably be best."

"Great. I'll see you a little before seven then."

"I'll be ready."

He drank the last of his juice. "I should be going." They walked together toward the locker rooms to change clothes.

"I guess I'll see you tonight," Tessa said at the door before going into the ladies' locker room.

Silas just smiled again and went into the men's.

Tessa showered and took her time dressing to let Silas leave first. After going back home, the rest of the day was a total waste for her. She couldn't concentrate on anything except the dinner. She did call Elaine to tell her they would both be there, and Elaine was thrilled Silas would be coming.

Late that afternoon, Tessa's nervousness got the best of her. She grabbed her phone and sat on the couch to call Sara.

"Hi Tessa, what's up?"

"Oh Sara, I think I've done something really stupid."

"What's wrong?"

"Silas accepted my invitation to the dinner at the neighbor's house tonight. What am I going to do?"

"You're going to go, that's what. What's wrong with you, girl?"

"I shouldn't have asked him. I don't even know him."

"Tessa, calm down. This isn't a date. It's just two people having dinner at the neighbor's house."

"I suppose you're right."

"Of course, I am. When am I ever wrong?"

Tessa laughed and started feeling a little better. "You always know the right thing to say. I couldn't have survived Colin's illness and his passing, if you hadn't been there with me. Thank you so much."

"That's what best friends are for."

"You're still coming down for Labor Day weekend, right?"

"I am. I reserved my flight today, and I'll email you the information as soon as I get home tonight. Now, go soak in a hot bath to relax and then get ready for your dinner and have fun."

"Thanks, Sara. I will." Tessa hung up the phone and took a deep breath. She did feel better now and got up to do just what Sara had said.

* * * * *

CHAPTER 2

TESSA sipped on a glass of wine to calm her nerves, until she heard his truck outside in her driveway and the door closing. She jumped up immediately and met him at the door just as he started to knock.

"Hi."

"Good evening."

She opened the door wider, and he stepped inside. As he moved past her, his aftershave lingered, nearly hypnotizing her. He had his hair pulled back in a ponytail and wore nice jeans and a blue long-sleeved buttoned shirt.

"You look nice," she said

"Thanks. You do too. I didn't know if you had something already, but I brought a bottle of wine to take to the Pratts' for dinner."

"I didn't even think of that. Thank you for remembering."

They both stood in the kitchen in an awkward moment.

"We probably should start over there," she suggested.

"Yes, we probably should."

He opened the door for her. They stepped out and walked across the road to the Pratts'. Silas knocked on the door, and Elaine opened it and greeted them.

"Hello, I'm so glad you both could make it. Please come in."

Silas placed his hand on Tessa's back as she stepped inside the house. To her surprise, at his touch, a warm feeling spread through her body, and her mouth turned up into just a hint of a smile.

"We brought this for you. I hope it goes well with the dinner," Silas said.

Elaine took the wine and looked at it. "It'll be perfect. Let me go put it on some ice. Dinner is almost ready."

"Can I help with anything?" Tessa asked.

"No, honey. I've got it all taken care of. Martin," Elaine called, "Silas and Tessa are here. Go on in the living room. He's watching some sort of game on television."

Tessa was amazed at the number of animal heads mounted to the walls and stuffed animals on the floor and shelves. "Did you hunt all of these?" she asked Martin as they entered the living room. He turned off the game.

"I did shoot most of the ones on the wall, but the others I purchased. I used to hunt a lot, but now I leave that to the younger bucks," Martin said. "You hunt, don't you, Silas?"

"Yes, sir."

"Would either of you like a drink?" he asked, getting up to pour himself another.

"Nothing for me. Thank you," Tessa said.

"I'll wait for dinner," Silas added.

"Please, sit down. Tessa, how do you like Tennessee so far?" Martin asked.

"I really like it. It's so beautiful and peaceful."

"Just wait a few weeks and it will all look totally different when the leaves have changed colors."

"Dinner is ready, if y'all want to come into the dining room," Elaine announced from the doorway.

Silas followed Tessa into the dining room and held her chair for her as she sat down. Elaine served the food, and Martin poured the wine. They all began eating.

"Silas, what do you think about that new regulation about using pistols to hunt deer?" Martin asked.

"I think it could make the woods more dangerous to be in, but for those that are good with pistols, it should be easy for them to get a deer."

"Which do you prefer to hunt with?"

"I'm still old school when it comes to hunting and like using a twelve-gauge shotgun."

"Honestly, I think you two need to go into another room to talk about your hunting. Tessa and I can't get a word in," Elaine said.

"I'm sorry, dear. You're right. Silas, are you taking on any new jobs right now? Elaine would like to add a room onto our house."

"I could probably do that for you, but it may be spring before I get to it. It will depend on our weather this winter. I have a few other jobs lined up that I'll have to do first, and I have to finish the shed across the street too." He looked at Tessa, who smiled and felt her face flush.

"I can wait, but give me a call soon so we can work out some details."

"I will."

Martin looked at Tessa. "Elaine tells me you're writing a book."

"It's really nothing. It's a mystery, but I've only just started the rough draft. Once I've finished writing it, there's editing to be done and then submitting to a publisher and hoping for it to be accepted. If it is, then it could take up to a year to get it published."

"That's interesting. I never knew it took so long," Martin said.

"If everyone is finished, how about we go into the living room and continue our conversation in there?" Elaine suggested.

Everyone was agreeable and stood. "Can I help clear the table?" Tessa asked.

"No, I'll take care of that later, but thanks," Elaine said.

Once in the living room, Martin sat in the large chair, and Elaine took the other, leaving the couch for Silas and Tessa. No one spoke for a few seconds.

"Would anyone care for a brandy?" Martin asked. "I'm going to have one. Silas?"

"Sure, why not," Silas said.

"Tessa?" Martin asked.

"I probably shouldn't after drinking the wine with dinner."

"Oh come on, one won't hurt. Have you ever had brandy before?"

"Actually, no. I usually stick to wine or an occasional beer with pizza."

"You must try the brandy that I have then. It's one of the best and a great after dinner drink." Martin poured two glasses and gave them to Silas and Tessa. "Darling?" He looked at Elaine.

"Yes, please," she replied.

After passing Elaine her glass, Martin turned and raised his. "A toast to new friends."

They all raised their glasses. Tessa only took a sip at first and found the drink to be smoother than she anticipated. Warmth spread throughout her body. She liked it.

The after dinner conversation went a variety of ways, from sports to hunting to the local government wanting to put a two-lane highway through Yellowwood to accommodate the increasing tourist traffic.

"It's been a great evening, but I think that maybe I should be going. I have some work to get to early in the morning. Tessa, are you ready?" Silas said.

"Yes, I should be going too." They all stood, with Tessa stumbling just a little. Silas caught her by the arm to steady her. "I'm so sorry. I didn't think I drank that much," she joked.

"That brandy can sneak up on you," Elaine said. "Silas, you will make sure she gets inside her home okay, won't you?"

"Yes, ma'am."

Silas held onto Tessa's arm as they walked to the front door to say their good-byes to the Pratts. On the walk to Tessa's cabin, he put his arm around her waist. She wondered if it was because he wanted to be closer or to keep her from tripping over her own feet. Either way, she liked the feel of him close to her.

At her door, she unlocked it and paused. "Would you like to come in?"

"Well, after you drank so much, I did promise Elaine I would make sure you got inside all right."

"Hey, I didn't drink that much." She playfully slapped him on the arm. "I'm just not used to it, especially the brandy." He held onto her hand as she stepped through the door ahead of him. "Would you like some coffee?"

"That sounds good, and I think we both could probably use some."

Thinking ahead, Tessa had already set up the coffeemaker. All she had to do was push the start button. When she turned back around, she found Silas standing right in front of her.

They looked into each other's eyes as he pulled her into his arms and kissed her. His lips were soft and cool, and she parted hers, allowing him in. His tongue made sweeping motions inside her mouth. He pulled her closer and deepened his kiss. She felt herself weaken in his embrace and was thankful he held her tight. The warm feeling she had from the brandy was nothing compared to being in his arms, but just as quickly as it started, Silas let go and took a step back.

"I'm sorry. I shouldn't have done that," he murmured.

"No, it's okay. I kind of liked it," she replied. She looked over at the coffeemaker to hide her embarrassment. "The coffee will be done soon. Do you want cream or sugar?" She turned back to the counter and opened the cabinet door.

"Black is fine. Tessa, I think we both had a little too much to drink tonight, and maybe we let our guard down. Again, I'm sorry."

She placed two cups on the counter next to the coffeemaker and then turned to him. "What if we have dinner together again, but this time with no alcohol and see what happens?"

Silas smiled. "That's a good idea, but I'm pretty sure I'm still going to want to kiss you."

"How does Sunday night work for you?"

"I have some work commitments tomorrow, but I think I can make it Sunday night."

"Okay then, it's a date. Now, how about that coffee?"

"I think under the circumstances, I had better take mine to go."

"Oh, okay." A little disappointed, she retrieved a travel mug from the cabinet and poured his coffee.

He took the mug from her and leaned in for a quick kiss on her cheek.

"See you Sunday night."

"Be careful driving home."

"I will. Bye."

He left, and she locked the door behind him, already thinking about their next dinner.

* * *

LATE Saturday afternoon, Tessa returned home from doing a little shopping for Sunday night's dinner and saw Silas' truck parked at the Pratts'. She assumed he was there talking about the room addition they wanted him to do. After carrying in the groceries and putting them away, she took the newspaper out to the backyard patio. She had almost finished reading when she heard a knock at her kitchen door. She stepped around the side of the house and saw Silas. "Hi, I'm back here."

He joined her on the patio. He was dressed from head to toe in camouflaged clothing, including his hat. His hair was again pulled back into a ponytail sticking out below his hat.

"I can only stay a few minutes, but wanted to apologize again for the way I acted last night," he said. "I'll understand if you want to cancel tomorrow night's dinner."

"Do you want to cancel the dinner?"

"No, not really."

"Neither do I. Let's just have a simple meal here at my place with no expectations and see how it goes."

"You're sure?"

"I'm looking forward to it," she replied. "Why are you dressed like that? Have you been hunting?"

"I, ah, well, ah, yes. I've been squirrel hunting."

"Didn't I see your truck at the Pratts'."

Before she could say anything more, his cell phone rang.

"Hello." He got up and turned away from her. "Okay. When?" He took a couple steps away. "Got it. Thanks." He hung up and turned back to her. "What time should I be here tomorrow night?"

"How about around six?"

"Perfect. I'll be here." He turned to leave.

"Wait." She grabbed a pen from the table next to her chair. She tore off a corner of the newspaper and wrote. "Here's my cell phone number, in case you need to call."

He took the paper and stuffed it into his pocket. "Thanks. See ya tomorrow night."

She walked with him to the front of the house. His truck was still parked at the Pratts' and as they said goodbye, Mae Nicholson turned her car into Tessa's driveway and got out.

"Hello, Mae," Tessa greeted her.

"Hello, dear. I thought I'd stop and pick up that basket I left the other day."

"Sure. I have it inside. Oh, Mae this is Silas Newberry. Silas, this is Mae Nicholson. She lives in that house just up the road from the Pratts."

Mae took a long gaze at him, looking him up and down. "You've been hunting?"

"Yes, ma'am."

"Hunting what?"

"Squirrels." He looked at Tessa.

"I'll see you tomorrow night, Silas," Tessa interrupted, giving Silas a way out of the conversation. Mae's questioning was probably making him uncomfortable.

Silas nodded, walked over to his truck, and left. Mae followed Tessa into the house to get the basket, and to Tessa's surprise, Mae sat down at the table. Apparently, she planned on visiting for a while.

"Here's your basket. Thank you again for the muffins. They were delicious." She picked it up from the counter and placed it on the table.

Mae pushed it aside. "Are you going out with that man?"

"Well, yes, sort of. He's coming for dinner tomorrow night." Tessa sat down at the table.

"You should keep your distance from him. He's up to no good."

"What makes you think that?"

"Those shotgun shells in his hunting vest were slugs," Mae said.

"I don't understand."

"You don't use slugs to hunt squirrels. There wouldn't be anything left. You use those to hunt bigger animals, like deer, bear, or elk."

"Okay, so maybe he's hunting bigger animals."

"The only hunting season in right now is squirrel. If he's hunting bigger animals, he's poaching."

"Maybe he just forgot to take those shells out of his vest."

"Or maybe he's working for Martin Pratt, illegally hunting game animals," Mae suggested.

"What? I don't understand."

"Haven't you noticed all the trucks and people going in and out of their house at all hours of the night?"

"No, I really haven't paid any attention."

"Maybe you should start, and I'd dump that boyfriend of yours before he gets you into the middle of something. You're too nice of a girl to get mixed up with someone like him. He's got a record, you know." Mae stood and picked up her basket. "Think about it." She turned and left the cabin.

Tessa was stunned. She went to the living room, sat on the couch, and started putting together the pieces in her mind. Silas had never told her anything about himself, didn't offer his phone number, and avoided telling her where he lived. Martin did have a lot of animal heads mounted in his house, and he and Silas talked a lot about hunting that night. Maybe there was something to what Mae said. She did seem like the type of person who would know everything that goes on in the neighborhood.

Confused, she picked up her laptop and went to one of those web sites where you can do a background check on someone to look for answers. With her credit card number, she punched in Silas' name. She couldn't believe what came up.

* * *

THE next evening, Silas arrived promptly at six o'clock. Tessa had decided to make things as casual as possible and dressed in jeans and a sweater. Silas also dressed casually, but she couldn't help noticing how well his tight T-shirt showed his taunt arm muscles.

She opened the door and hesitated only for a second. "Good evening. Please come in."

He entered and took in a deep breath. "Wow, something smells really good."

"I made fried chicken, mashed potatoes, and green beans. Everything is already done and in the oven to keep warm. We can eat whenever you want."

"I'm starved right now."

"Sit down and I'll get everything out," she said. "What would you like to drink? I have soda, sweet tea, or I could make some coffee."

"Soda is fine. Let me help you?" He started to get up from the table.

"No, I can do it."

She brought the food and drinks to the table that was already set and sat down next to him.

"How's your book coming along?" he asked.

"I guess it's going well."

"Why did you decide to come to Tennessee to write?" he asked.

"Colin, that was my husband, and I always talked about coming here on a vacation. But our teaching schedules never gave us the time. After his passing, and once I decided to take a break from teaching, this was the only place I could think of going. He would have loved it here with all the history of the area."

Silas looked down and took a bite of food.

Tessa blurted out, "I'm sorry. I shouldn't have brought him up."

"It's fine. It sounds like he was a great guy."

Tessa concentrated on her food. This wasn't going as well as she had hoped.

"This food's really good," he said.

"Thanks. I do like to cook, but I don't get much of a chance to cook a big meal living alone. I mostly just eat soups and salads, but it was fun to cook a whole meal again."

"I suppose you like teaching at the college level?"

"I do like it. For the most part, the students are there because they want to be, but every once in a while you get a prankster or someone mixed up in something they shouldn't be." It left her mouth before she could think.

"I guess college kids do get into stuff they shouldn't," he replied.

She talked a little more about teaching, and before long, they had finished their meal.

"Let me clear these dishes. I made chocolate cake for dessert."

"Chocolate cake, that's my favorite, but only a small piece. I'm stuffed."

"I can keep it fresh, and you can have some for lunch when you're here working this week."

"That's a great idea."

She brought them both a slice of cake and some coffee. He took a bite. "Oh my God, this is the best cake I think I've ever tasted. What did you do to make it so good?"

"A cook never tells her secrets," she replied. Silas smiled, and she melted quicker than the icing on the cake.

"I know you told Martin that you liked living here. Was that the truth?" he asked.

"Yes. Why would I lie?"

"I thought maybe you were just being nice."

"Maybe I'm just being nice to you now."

He cocked his head and looked at her. "No, I think you're probably telling the truth."

"You think you can read me that well?"

"I'm pretty good at reading people."

She smiled at him. "I guess you are. I like it here more and more each day."

"Some of the views around here are unbelievable. There's this one spot along a trail in the park that I'll have to take you to. It's breathtaking early in the morning."

"That sounds great. I love to go hiking."

"Would you like to go tomorrow? I know the leaves haven't turned yet, but there are some wonderful views of the mountains."

Surprised by the sudden invitation, she accepted before even thinking about it. "Yes, but don't you have to work?"

"We can go early in the morning before work or later in the afternoon after I finish for the day. Either would be fine with me."

"Later in the afternoon would be better for me, I think."

"Would around four o'clock be okay?"

"That would be perfect."

"Good." He took a drink of his coffee." You know, there's a full moon out tonight. Would you like to go outside and take a look?"

She smiled. "Sure."

Silas took her hand and they went out to the backyard. Even in August, the night was a bit cool in the mountains. "Let me start a fire in the pit," he said.

"Okay, but won't that make it harder to see the night sky?"

"Yes, but that's not the real reason I wanted to come out here."

Tessa sat down on the outdoor sectional and after he got the fire burning, he joined her and put his arm around her.

They sat there for several minutes and in the calmness, they started to hear sounds of the night. "Listen to that," he said.

"What?"

"It sounds like someone screaming, but it's really a screech owl way out in the woods."

"Oh, I hear it now."

"Be real quiet and listen. Tell me what else you hear."

They sat in silence and listened.

"I hear crickets and another kind of bird. What is that?" she asked.

"It's a whip-poor-will. You've never heard a whip-poor-will before?"

"I'm a city girl."

"I kind of like city girls." Silas leaned over and gave her a quick kiss on the cheek. "Tessa, the kiss we had the other night was not just the alcohol." He placed his hand on her chin to turn her face toward him and kissed her again. His tongue slipped between her lips, and he pulled her closer. His hand on her thigh moved upward, under her sweater. She kissed him back.

Then, it happened. The worst thing that possible could, his cell phone rang. He let out a breath and sat back on the sectional. Pulling his phone out of his pocket, he looked at the display. "Sorry, I have to answer this." He stood up and walked a few steps away from her. "Hello."

Tessa strained to hear what he was saying, but had no luck.

He quickly hung up the phone and sat back down next to her. He brushed a strand of hair off of her forehead. "I have to go. Could we maybe continue this on another night?"

"I don't know." She hesitated. "Silas, I should tell you that I have trust issues with you."

"I don't understand."

"You never talk about yourself. Our whole conversation over dinner this evening was about me. You won't tell me where you live or even give me your phone number. It's like you're hiding something from me." She knew she said too much, but once she started she couldn't stop.

Silas sat back and took a deep breath, letting it out slowly. "My life is very complicated right now. I really can't go into it, but I'm not married and I don't have a girlfriend. I value my privacy and letting someone in takes a little time." His cell phone beeped with a text message. "I really need to go," he said after checking it, "but please know that I am interested in seeing if this might be something more than just a friendship between us."

Tessa stood and followed him to his truck. Silas put his arms around her and kissed her deeply again. "Are we still on for that hike tomorrow?"

"Yes."

"I'll see you around four o'clock then." He got in his truck and started the engine.

She stepped away when he backed out of her driveway.

Tessa walked back into her house only to hear another car engine start outside.

She looked out the window and saw a car leave the Pratts' house. Mae had said people were coming and going all night from their house. She wondered if that call Silas received had anything to do with the Pratts.

* * *

WHEN Silas arrived the next day for their hike, she didn't even give him a chance to come inside. As soon as she saw him pull in the driveway, she grabbed her small backpack, went outside, and jumped into his truck. "Hi."

"Hello. Ready to tackle the trails today?" he asked.

"I can't wait."

"Did you bring a camera? There will be some great spots for pictures."

"I did. Where are we going?"

He pulled the truck out onto the road and heading toward the park. "I'm taking you to the Grotto Falls trail. It's about a two and a half mile hike. Feel up to that?"

"Piece of cake."

He looked at her feet. "New boots?"

"I know what you're going to say. I shouldn't be wearing new boots on a long hike. These really aren't new. I bought them about a year ago, but just haven't worn them much. I was part of a hiking club at the university, and it seemed like most of the time when they planned a hike, I had something else to do."

"There's hiking in Illinois?" he teased.

"Yes, there is. We have some great places to hike."

"I bet they won't be anything like what you'll see today."

It took about twenty minutes to get to the parking area near the trailhead. Silas pulled the truck to a stop, and they both got out. "I brought some bottles of water for us," he said as he got his pack out of the backseat of the truck.

"That's good because it's really warm today."

With the parking lot about half full, the trail was probably fairly busy too. "This is one of the more popular trails in the park. Looks like we'll probably run into several other hikers today."

At the trailhead, Tessa stopped for a minute to read a sign warning of bears in the area. "There are bear around here?"

"They're all through the park. If we're careful and pay attention to our surroundings, we'll be fine. You don't have any food in your pack, do you?"

"No, just my camera and my purse."

"I'm sure we'll be fine then. Let's go." He took her hand, and they headed up the trail.

The first thing she noticed was the large evergreen type trees lining the trail. "What kind of trees are those?"

"They're hemlock trees."

"Like the poison in the Romeo and Juliet play?"

"No, that poison comes from the Hemlock plant. Hemlock trees are not the same thing."

"You sure know a lot about the outdoors."

"I spent most of my life in the woods. You learn a lot doing that."

After getting past the trees, a beautiful stream trickled along side the trail. Tessa stopped several times to take pictures. She could hear the sound of loud rushing water echoing ahead of them. "Are we close to the falls?"

"Not as close as you would think. There's a small waterfall up ahead, but it's not the main one."

They continued on their hike, and in a few places along the trail, they had to cross small streams without the benefit of a bridge. Silas held her hand tightly as they stepped on the wet stones to cross. The last thing she wanted to do was fall on her butt and have to finish the hike in wet clothes, not to mention how embarrassed she'd be in front of Silas.

A tumbling cascade came into view as they made their way up the trail. "This is so pretty. I need to take some pictures."

"Okay, but we need to get going if we want to see Grotto Falls and make it back to the truck before it gets too dark," he said.

After snapping a few pictures, they took off again. Soon she could hear more water ahead of them, and then the main waterfall came into view. "Is that it?"

"That's it."

"It's beautiful."

It took another twenty minutes for them to actually reach the waterfall by the trail. The water plunged over the edge of the rock into a white cascade of water before ending in the pool below.

"There's a trail that runs behind the fall, if you'd like to go down there," he said.

"Oh yes. That would be great."

They met several other hikers coming up from the waterfall as they made their way down. The spray of the twenty-five foot waterfall cooled her face as they walked behind it. The ground was wet and slippery, but Silas kept a good hold of her so she wouldn't fall.

"This is so cool," she said while standing behind the waterfall and feeling the thunderous power of the water as it hit the ground. The spray felt cool on her face.

"There's some rocks over there we can sit on if you want to stick your feet in," he said over the sound of the rushing water.

She nodded her head yes, and he led her over. They both took their socks and shoes off and stuck their feet into the cool mountain water.

"How do your feet feel?" he asked.

"They're a little sore, but the water feels good on them. It's so pretty here."

"I think so too."

She looked over at him and caught him staring at her. He smiled and blushed.

As the sun lowered in the sky, Silas suggested they head back. With their socks and shoes back on, they started their hike. He held her hand the whole way. Once they reached his truck, he opened the door for her, but before he helped her into the truck, he cupped her chin and kissed her. He then got in, and they drove back to her house.

"I'll probably be sore tomorrow from the hike."

"I'm available for massages," Silas said.

"Yeah, but are you any good?"

"I've been told that I'm very good." He raised his eyebrow and gave her a little smile.

"I just bet you are." Tessa began daydreaming about how his hands would feel on her naked body, starting with her feet and working his way up. A warm feeling began at the apex of her legs and radiated throughout her body. She smiled.

"What are you smiling at?"

"Oh nothing, I just thought about how great this day has been." Her face grew warm.

When they arrived back at her cabin, Silas walked her to the door.

"This was the best time I've had in a long time. It really got my heart pumping. Thank you for taking me," she said.

"It was my pleasure. I had a great time too." He took a step toward her.

"Would you like to come in? I could probably find something to fix for supper."

"I would really like to, but I think I should go. If I came in, I'm not sure I could make myself leave." He took another stepped toward her, and they were so close that they were nearly touching.

"Another time, then," she whispered.

"I certainly hope so." He leaned down, and their lips came together. This wasn't just any kiss, but a full on exploratory and intoxicating kiss.

"Wow," she murmured when they parted.

"Until next time." He tipped his head and walked back to his truck.

Still thinking about that kiss, she wasn't sure she was going to make it inside the house before her knees gave out. It was that good. She would have no trouble falling asleep tonight and hoped her dreams would be filled with Silas.

* * *

THE next afternoon, Tessa sat at her computer working on her book when she heard a vehicle pull into her driveway.

She looked out the window and saw Silas getting his toolbox out of the bed of the truck. She quickly ran to the bathroom to run a comb through her hair and apply just a touch of lipstick. By the time she came back out, he had already walked past the house and was out back at the garage. She needed to come up with an excuse to go out and see him. She sat down at the kitchen table to think. The sound of the saw running didn't help her concentration. Wait, she hadn't told him about the cookout on Labor Day!

As she walked out, Silas looked up, saw her coming, and turned off the saw. "Hi." His ocean blue eyes nearly made her forget what she was out there for.

"Hi. How are you this afternoon?" she said.

"I'm good. I wanted to try and catch up on some of my work. I had some things to do this morning and couldn't make it here until now. Are you sore from our hike?"

"Just a little stiff maybe. I forgot to ask you something yesterday." She took a sharp inhale so she could say it all in one go. "My friend Sara is coming to visit over Labor Day weekend, and I wanted to have a cookout on that Sunday afternoon so she could meet some of my friends down here. I was hoping you could come."

"I'd love to. Thanks."

"I also have a favor to ask. I don't have a grill and didn't want to buy one since I'm only here for a year. Do you have a grill I could use?"

"I think I can manage to find one, but on one condition," he said.

"What's that?"

"Let me do the grilling?"

"Sure, as long as you're good at it. That would be great."

"I'm great at grilling."

"Oh, do you have a friend that you could bring too?"

"A friend?"

"I mean a guy friend" she said, a little flustered, "so Sara won't be the odd numbered person."

"Let me see, a grill and a friend. Most people are asked to just bring a side dish," he teased.

"Very funny. I'm asking the Pratts too."

His expression darkened a shade. "The Pratts."

"Yes, since they asked us to dinner, I thought I'd return the favor," she said.

"Sure, that's a good idea, and I have the perfect friend to bring. I think both you and your friend will like him."

Silas' cell phone rang. He pulled it out of his pocket and looked at it. "I need to take this." He stepped around the side of the shed.

She strained to hear his conversation, but all she could make out were mumbles. Her mind drifted back to Mae's accusation that Silas was involved with poaching animals for Martin Pratt. She couldn't help but think all these phone calls were somehow connected. She heard him end the call and come back around to her.

"I'm sorry about that. So, do I need to bring anything else for this cookout?"

"No, just your friend and the grill will be fine. I probably should let you get back to your work. Will you be here tomorrow?"

"As far as I know, I will."

Tessa smiled and went back into her house. She was standing at the open kitchen window when she saw Silas take out his phone to make a call. He stood nearly under the window and must not have noticed it was open. This allowed Tessa to hear his side of the conversation.

"Hi. It's Silas. I'm going to need a couple salt blocks for tonight. Can you put two out for me?"

She leaned closer to the window to try and hear better.

"Right. Can you have them out in about thirty minutes? Great. Thanks." He ended the call and went back to work.

Even she knew salt blocks weren't used to hunt squirrels. Enough of this. She went to the bedroom to change. Rummaging through her closet, she searched for appropriate clothes for her mission. She pulled out a chambray shirt and a pair of old jeans. From the bottom of her closet, she picked up her tennis shoes and sat on the bed to put them on.

This is the craziest idea I've ever had. I should trust Silas.

Deciding against her idea, she started to take her shoe off, but hesitated. If he's into something bad, she needed to know about it. Even if it turns out to be nothing, it could make for a great scene in her book.

Twenty minutes later, she slipped out the front door and looked up and down the street, especially over toward the Pratts'. With the coast clear, she climbed up in the bed of Silas' truck and hid herself under one of the tarps.

What was that smell? It was going to make her sick. She heard footsteps coming toward the truck. Suddenly, something landed with a thud on the truck bed next to her. Silas had dropped his toolbox there, nearly landing on top of her. She felt him get into the truck and close the door. The engine started, and he backed out of the driveway. The truck sped up as he drove down the road.

Several minutes later, she felt the truck stopped, and Silas get out. "Hey, how's it going?" he said to someone.

"You sure you only need two blocks?"

"Yeah, that'll do this time. Here's your money. Thanks."

He put something in the bed of the truck back next to the tailgate and got back into the truck and drove off. Tessa could tell he was driving up into the mountains, but she had no idea where they were. She moved the tarp aside and looked up, but all she could see were trees and tall mountains. She did, however, see that the things he had put in the truck were in fact salt blocks. Then, he turned onto a bumpy road that nearly shook her right out of the truck.

Finally, Silas stopped the truck, got out, and unloaded the salt blocks. Before he got back into the truck, something tickled her nose. She tried to hold a sneeze in, but couldn't.

"Ah-choo!"

The tarp suddenly came off, and Silas stared down at her, shocked. "What the hell are you doing there?"

"I'm sorry, but I had to know what you were doing?" She sat up.

"What do you mean you had to know what I was doing?"

"Mae Nicholson told me that you were messing around with some illegal stuff with Martin Pratt."

"She did, did she? And, you believed her?"

"Not entirely. That's why I hid in here, so I could see for myself."

"Come on down from there. I'm taking you home." She stood up, and he helped her down out of the back of the truck.

She walked around to the passenger side and got in. Silas was already sitting in the driver's seat and had the truck started. As soon as she buckled in, he took off. That surly expression was back on his face as he stared straight ahead. He didn't say a word on the drive back. She had never seen him, or anyone for that matter, so furious.

"I'm sorry," she said again.

"Just how were you planning on getting back home, if I hadn't found you?"

"I don't know. I hadn't really thought that far ahead."

"Brilliant."

"What were the salt blocks for? Are you really baiting animals?"

He didn't answer right away. "I was baiting animals, but not for what you think. The Visitors Center in the park conducts photography tours through here, and they pay me to put salt blocks out for the deer and elk. When they bring the people through with their cameras, there's a better chance of getting some pictures of the animals if they've been baited."

"That's it? You're doing it for the Park Service?"

"That's it."

She relaxed into the seat. "I'm sorry again."

"Next time, just ask me."

"I will." She wasn't sure she totally believed him, but she wasn't going to let him know that she still had doubts.

* * * * *

CHAPTER 3

Two weeks later

TESSA only had two days to wait before Sara would be arriving to spend Labor Day weekend with her. Silas had almost finished with the shed and already had other jobs lined up afterward. In the last couple weeks, they had gone out to dinner a few times, and she purposely had not asked him any personal questions, and he still didn't volunteer any information about himself.

It was getting late in the day, and after stocking the pantry for the weekend cookout, she worked on her book for most of the afternoon. Earlier, Silas had told her about wild blackberry bushes in the woods behind her cabin, and she wanted to pick some berries for a cobbler she planned to bake for the cookout.

After finding a plastic bag in the kitchen drawer, she strolled down the lightly used trail to get the berries. She had been picking berries for about fifteen minutes when she thought she heard a stick snap behind her. She looked around, but didn't see anything. She heard it again. This time she looked to her right and saw a huge black bear. Apparently, he considered this his berry bush and didn't want to share. Tessa stopped picking and started to slowly step backward away from the bear, but it kept walking toward her, grunting and moving a little faster with each step.

Her heart raced as she stepped back faster. She tried to think of what to do. Panic began to set in when the bear moved faster and growled at her. Finally, she dropped the bag of berries and turned to run back toward the cabin. After only a few steps, she tripped on a tree root and fell to the ground. She screamed as the bear stood above her and started pushing her around on the ground with its front paws. Tessa, curled herself up into a ball as small as she could, arms covering her head. Its claws scratched her arms as she tried to protect her face. She kept screaming for help and praying for the bear to stop.

Suddenly, a shot rang out and then another and another until the bear stopped and fell to the ground. Trembling, she felt something pulling at her arms and then heard a voice.

"Tessa, Tessa, it's me. Are you okay?" She finally realized the voice belonged to Silas. He picked her up, and she wrapped her arms around him. She couldn't speak, only cried, while he carried her back to the cabin. Inside, he took her into the bathroom and sat her next to the sink.

He lifted her chin to look straight at her. "I need to clean you up to see how bad you're hurt."

She nodded her head, tears running down her face. She felt like she was in a fog, numb and confused about what had happened.

"Tessa, where do you hurt?"

She still couldn't answer.

She watched as he took off his long-sleeved jacket and saw that he wore a handgun in a holster under his arm. His attention back to her, he slowly unbuttoned and removed her shirt to check her arms and gently washed them with a warm damp cloth.

"It looks like its just some scratches, but I really need to get the wounds cleaned. I'm going to have to put you in the shower because you have scratches all over your body."

She nodded her head. Her sobbing had subsided, but she still felt tears swelling in her eyes. He turned on the shower and after a few minutes the steam started rolling. He removed the rest of her clothes and lifted her off the counter. They both stepped into the shower, him fully clothed.

Silas gently washed the blood from her wounds, careful not to touch her sensitive areas. "It doesn't look bad at all," he said. "You have some deep scratches, but I'll bandage them, and I think you'll be fine." She wrapped her arms around him and laid her head against his chest. He held her tight.

The warm water running down her body felt good, but his arms around her felt even better. After a few minutes, he turned off the water, wrapped a large soft towel around her, and they both stepped out of the shower. As softly as he could, he padded her dry and then helped her with her robe and bandaged her wounds. After finishing with the bandages, he put his arm around her waist and led her to the bedroom where she slowly crawled into bed. Silas pulled the blankets up over her and started to leave the room.

"Don't go," she called after him.

"I'm just going to dry myself off. I'll be back in a few minutes."

In a short time, he walked back into the bedroom wearing only a towel. He placed his cell phone and his gun on the table next to the bed and crawled in beside her, taking her into his arms. She laid her head on his chest, placing her hand over his heart. His smooth chest was warm, and she could hear his heart beating.

Silas kissed the top of her head. "You're going to be fine," he whispered.

"I was so scared."

"I know."

"Did you kill the bear?"

"Yes."

"Good." She looked up at him. "Thank you for saving my life."

He leaned down and kissed her, but it was so much more. His hand felt rough against her smooth skin when he lightly caressed her face. She moved up closer to him, kissing him deeply and inviting him for more. Loosing her robe, his hand found her breast already grown into a hard peak. She groaned when he touched her.

"I'm sorry. Did I hurt you?" he asked.

"No."

"I don't want to hurt you."

"You aren't. I want this."

Silas rolled her onto her back and took her nipple into his mouth. She arched her back in response. He moved from one breast to the other and then worked his kisses back up to the neck. She shivered when he reached her earlobe.

She made good use of her hands by letting them roam over his hard muscles. She heard his breathing increase as she moved closer to his member until she took him into her hand and gently massaged his growing erection.

"Tessa, I'll be as gentle as I can, but I can't wait any longer."

"You're not going to hurt me," she whispered back.

He rolled on top and as gently as he could, eased into her. The sensation of him inside nearly sent her over the edge immediately. She quickly fell into his rhythm, and they slowly began rocking together until they achieved a sweet simultaneous climax. They both gasped for breath as he rolled off of her to let her breathe easier.

"I didn't hurt you, did I?" he asked.

"No. It was perfect." She moved over next to him, and he put his arm around her. She looked up and kissed him, then laying her head back on his chest, fell asleep.

A few hours later, Tessa felt Silas slip out of bed. She didn't say anything, thinking he was probably just going to the bathroom. She opened her eyes just in time to spy his naked butt walking out of the room, but then she noticed he carried his cell phone in his hand. The house was quiet, and she tried to hear his conversation, but the only thing she could make out was that he wasn't going to make a meeting tonight. Then, she heard the kitchen door open and close.

A few minutes later, she heard the door open and close again and footsteps coming toward the bedroom. He returned wearing a pair of runner's shorts and climbed back into bed next to her. He put his arm around her again, and she soon felt his breathing slow. He had fallen asleep, and it didn't take long for her to fall asleep too.

* * *

TESSA woke up the next morning and rolled over to find herself alone in bed with the aroma of coffee tickling her nose.

She climbed out of bed, but the soreness of her muscles slowed her movement. It seemed as though every muscle in her body ached. Once standing, she got a pair of panties out of the dresser and put them on, followed by her robe. Steadying herself by holding onto the wall, she slowly walked to the kitchen, but Silas wasn't there. She looked in the living room and then went to the kitchen door and saw him outside talking on his cell phone. When he looked up and saw her, he ended the call and came back inside.

"Good morning," he said. "How are you feeling?"

"I'm really sore and have a headache."

He took her hand and slid the sleeve of her robe up to examine the bandages on her arm. "I need to clean and bandage your arms again."

"I can do it. I can take care of myself today."

"Let me, please. I want to check your wounds for infection."

They walked down the hallway to the bathroom.

Standing next to the sink, Silas slowly peeled off the bandages. The blood had dried into a dark brown color and removing a few of the bandages caused the wounds to start bleeding a little again. "They look fine. I don't see any signs of infection, but you should go to the clinic in town and get checked out. You may need a tetanus shot."

"How do you know so much?"

"I learned a lot in the Army."

Silas put some antiseptic ointment on the bandages to keep them from sticking to the wound and applied the new bandages. When he finished, he gave her a quick kiss. "All done."

They left the bathroom and headed back toward the kitchen.

"I'm going to change my clothes. I'll be out in a few minutes," she said.

"While you do that, I'll start some breakfast."

When she returned to the kitchen, Silas brought her a cup of coffee, placed two plates of eggs and bacon on the table for them, and then sat down with her.

"I brought in your bag of blackberries from last night," he said, taking a bite of egg.

"Going out there was the dumbest thing I've ever done." She picked at her food.

"You had no way of knowing there'd be a bear out there."

"No, but you told me to be careful because they were around, and I didn't even think about that." She took a sip of coffee. "Is the bear still out there?"

"No."

"Where is it?"

"I took care of it. Don't worry about it."

"Why do you carry a gun?" she asked.

"Luckily for you, I was carrying it last night."

"You carry one all the time?"

"Yes."

"Why?"

"You sure ask a lot of questions." He got up and took his plate to the sink. "I need to go. I have to go home and change clothes before going to work. Do you need me to do anything before I leave?"

"No." Tessa noted his avoidance about carrying a gun. She got up and walked to the door with him.

He turned back to her before going out the door. "I hope what we did last night was okay, and I didn't hurt you."

"You didn't hurt me. Other than the bear attack, everything last night was absolutely perfect. Will you be back tonight?"

"No. You need to rest, and I have some things to do. I probably won't be back until the Sunday cookout when your friend is here."

She was disappointed. "Sara arrives tomorrow and don't forget to bring a friend, so she won't be the odd person."

"I promise." Silas gave her a kiss and left.

Later that afternoon, Tessa heard someone knocking and went to the door. "Hi, Elaine. Come in."

"I just wanted to stop by and see how you're feeling."

"What do you mean?"

"The bear attack. It must have been terrifying." Elaine looked at Tessa's bandaged arms.

"How did you know?" Tessa asked.

"I, well, I, ah, Martin saw Silas in town earlier. He told him, and I was up last night getting a drink of water when I saw Silas come out of your house wearing nothing but a towel. I must say he has an impressive physique."

Tessa blushed. "Silas stayed to make sure I was okay. I only have some scratches. He said the bear was just playing with me." She needed to change the subject. "Oh, don't forget about the cookout on Sunday. My friend Sara will be here, and Silas will be grilling burgers."

"We're looking forward to it. I should go and let you get some rest. I just wanted to look in on you. You must be exhausted after your ordeal."

"I am pretty sore, but I'm fine. Although, taking it easy today does sound like a good idea. Thanks for checking on me."

"You're welcome, dear. I'll see you on Sunday. If you need anything, let me know." Elaine left, and Tessa decided to lie down on the couch for a while and, as she had told Elaine, spend the rest of the day taking it easy watching television.

Around four o'clock the following day, Tessa looked out the window with her cell phone to her ear. "You made the turn? Good, now come up the hill, and my cabin is on the right. Oh, I see you. I'll be right out." She hung up and walked outside as fast as her sore body would allow and gave Sara a hug after she got out of the car.

Taking a step back, Tessa looked at Sara. Already in awe of her beauty, Sara hadn't changed. Her long, dark, shiny copper colored hair was perfect and not a hair out of place. The jeans and green sweater that matched her eyes showed off her perfectly curved body that Tessa always envied.

"You look fantastic. How was your flight down?"

"It was good."

"I wish you would have let me pick you up at the airport instead of you renting a car."

"I enjoyed the drive. It's so beautiful down here."

"I know. Aren't the leaves gorgeous? We'll take a drive tomorrow, and I'll show you around, but let's get your bags and go inside."

Sara opened the trunk and lifted two bags out. She gave Tessa the smaller one to carry, and they started into the cabin. "Tessa, why are you moving so slow? You always left me in your tracks when we walked on campus. Has living down here made you lazy?" her friend teased.

"Come in the house and I'll tell you all about it."

Once inside, they put the bags down, and Tessa got them both a glass of sweet tea. They sat at the kitchen table to talk. She pulled up her long sleeves and revealed her bandaged arms to Sara.

"Oh my gosh, what happened?" Sara asked.

"I was attacked by a bear."

"A bear!" Her eyes widened. "Are you okay?"

"I'm fine." She pulled the sleeves back down and explained what happened and how Silas had shot the bear.

"He saved your life."

"Yes, he probably did."

"When do I get to meet this hero?"

"He'll be here for the cookout on Sunday." She stood up and got some cookies from the cabinet.

"Tessa, is there something else wrong?"

"I don't know. There's so much about him that he won't tell me. One minute he's this wonderful, caring man and then the next minute, he's back to the secrets, getting mysterious phone calls or texts, and then he has to leave."

"What does your heart tell you?"

"I've fallen for him really hard, and that it may be a mistake."

"Why a mistake?"

"I did one of those Internet background checks on him."

"And?"

She took a deep breath and let it out. "Silas has a criminal record. He was arrested in Virginia for poaching bear, theft, tampering with evidence, and aggravated assault with a weapon. He served a prison sentence and was released a little over a year ago. He's a felon."

"I understand how you think a relationship could be a mistake, but as far as you know he hasn't been in any trouble since his release, right?"

"I don't think so. At least nothing showed up on that criminal history search."

"So maybe he's changed," Sara said.

"Maybe he hasn't got caught yet."

"Why would you say that?"

"My little neighbor lady up the road thinks he's mixed up with the people across the street doing some sort of illegal poaching. After she told me that, I've been watching, and she may be right."

"Why don't you just ask him?"

"I couldn't do that. I don't have the right to."

"Tessa, have you slept with him?"

She hesitated. "Yes, but only once."

"You care about him. You have the right to ask."

"Maybe so. Oh, I don't know."

"You don't have to do it now. Enjoy the holiday weekend and then decide what to do," Sara suggested.

"That sounds like a plan. Hey, are you hungry? I could order a pizza, and I have a bottle of wine in the refrigerator to go with it."

"That sounds really good, and I am hungry."

Tessa ordered pizza, and they talked a little more over the bottle of wine. Several hours later, they decided to call it a night. "Look at the time. You must be exhausted after your flight today. We better get some sleep," Tessa said.

"Yeah, I am kinda tired, and I'm feeling the effects of that wine."

Tessa and Sara took the luggage to the extra bedroom, and Tessa showed her where the towels were for a shower.

"I'm so glad you're here, Sara. See you in the morning." The two friends hugged before heading to their bedrooms.

* * *

THE next day, Tessa took Sara on a sightseeing drive through the park to look at the beautiful views of the fall foliage.

With traffic being heavy since it was peak leaf season, it took most of the day just to go to all the best viewing spots. After finally leaving the park, they stopped in town to get a few last minute things for tomorrow's cookout. The last stop they needed to make before returning home was at the liquor store. Finding a parking place in town was just as bad as the traffic in the park. Tessa eyed an empty parking spot and took it before someone else.

After making their purchases, they walked out and loaded the car, but Tessa noticed something on the other side of the road. "That's Silas over there."

Both ladies looked across the street to the hardware store parking lot. Silas stood next to his truck talking to another man. They were too far away to hear what was being said, but it was obvious they were having a disagreement. Suddenly, the other man pushed Silas, who grabbed the guy by the shirt collar, pulling him closer and saying something to him. After releasing him, the man got in his truck and peeled out of the parking lot. Silas did the same going the opposite direction.

"What was that all about?" Sara asked.

"More of his mysterious side. I could ask him about it, but he won't tell me."

After a long day of sightseeing and shopping, the ladies drove back to Tessa's cabin to start getting things ready for tomorrow's cookout.

Sunday finally arrived and the Pratts were the first to arrive. "Welcome, let me take that for you," Tessa said, taking the casserole dish from Elaine. "There are drinks in the cooler over there. Sara, this is Elaine and Martin Pratt who live across the street. This is my best friend Sara that I worked with at the university."

"It's nice to meet you," Elaine said, lightly shaking Sara's hand.

"Nice to meet you too. Tessa has told me how welcomed you've made her."

"We're happy to have such a good neighbor," Martin said, then headed over to the cooler.

"Can I help with anything?" Elaine offered.

"I have everything in the kitchen. As soon as Silas gets here, he'll start grilling the burgers. Should I put this in the refrigerator?" Tessa asked referring to the casserole dish.

"You can leave it on the counter for now. It's mac and cheese and doesn't need refrigerating until after we eat."

"Please have a seat and I'll take it inside. I don't know what's keeping Silas."

Sara and the Pratts sat at the umbrella-shaded table while Tessa took the food into the house.

Silas arrived a little later and did bring a friend with him. Tessa was relieved to see him walk up. "It's about time. I was beginning to get worried," she said.

"Something came up," he whispered to her as he kissed her cheek.

"Hi everyone, this is my buddy, Austin Drake. Sorry we're late. We had a couple things to do before we could come."

Austin looked the opposite of Silas, standing a little taller with short light brown hair, brown eyes, and what looked like a three-day growth of beard. All in all, a great looking guy with a sweet smile.

"Hi, Austin. It's nice to meet you. I'm Tessa. That's Martin and Elaine Pratt, who live across the street, and this is Sara, my friend visiting from Illinois."

"Hello, everyone."

"Austin, help yourself to a beer in the cooler," Tessa said.

"Thanks." He walked over to the cooler.

Silas took Tessa by the hand and pulled her into the kitchen. Once inside he gave her a hug and kiss.

"I need to start taking the food outside. You brought your grill, didn't you?" Tessa walked away from him.

"Yes. Tessa, what's wrong?"

"Nothing." She kept herself busy getting things out of the refrigerator.

He gently grabbed her wrist turning her toward him. *"What is wrong?"*

Tessa looked down at his hand on her wrist, and he released her. "Sara and I were in town today, and we saw you arguing with some guy in the hardware store parking lot. You grabbed his shirt, and it looked like you were going to hit him."

He stepped back away from her. "That guy had cheated me in a deal. Yeah, I was kind of mad, but everything is fine now. I talked to him later and he made good on our deal. There's nothing to worry about."

"You're sure?"

"Positive. Are we okay now?"

"We're okay." She wasn't, but didn't want it to ruin the day.

"Good." Silas stepped toward her again and kissed her gently on the lips.

"Can I help?" Sara walked through the door. "Oops, sorry,"

"It's okay. Silas, this is Sara Brock, my best friend visiting from home."

"Hello, Sara. Tessa talks non-stop about you. I'm glad we finally got to meet," Silas said, extending his hand.

She shook his hand. "Me too and I've heard a lot about you too."

"I hope it was all good."

"You have nothing to worry about." Sara picked up the paper plates and napkins and went back outside.

"I guess I better get the grill unloaded from the truck and start cooking those burgers." He stopped before going out the door. "What did you tell Sara about me?"

"You have your secrets, and I have mine," Tessa said as she walked past him and out the door.

Silas and Austin unloaded the grill and before long, the burgers were sizzling over the heat. Tessa and Sara went back into the kitchen to get more ice and beer for the cooler.

"I really like Silas, and he's gorgeous," Sara said.

"He is, isn't he? I'm glad you like him."

"Did you ask him about what we saw yesterday in the parking lot?"

"He made up some excuse about the guy cheating him in a deal, but I don't believe him. Something wasn't right about his story."

"What do you mean?"

Before Tessa could answer, Silas walked into the kitchen. "The burgers are almost done. Can I help you bring the rest of the food out?"

Sara picked up the mac and cheese Elaine brought and carried it outside.

"Here, take this out for me." She handed Silas a dish of baked beans and then heard a knock. They both looked at the door.

"Mae, I didn't think you were going to come." Tessa opened the door and let the older lady, carrying a bowl of watermelon, step inside.

"I wouldn't have missed this for the world, dear." She looked at Silas.

"Mae, you remember Silas Newberry."

"It's nice to see you again, ma'am." Silas nodded to the lady.

Mae looked Silas up and down, paying particular attention to his long hair. "You need a haircut."

"Yes, ma'am. I hear that a lot. I better take this out and make sure Austin isn't over-cooking the burgers." Silas backed out the door making a funny face behind Mae's back to Tessa.

"Let me take that for you. Everyone is out in the backyard," Tessa said, trying not to laugh at Silas.

Tessa showed Mae outside and introduced her to Sara and Austin.

Silas finished the burgers and sat the platter on the table in front of everyone. He took his seat next to Tessa, and everyone dug into the food.

"Tessa, how is your book coming along?" Elaine asked.

"Not too bad. I have a rough draft of at least two chapters finished."

"Book? What are you writing?" Austin asked.

"It's a mystery that takes place in the mountains of Tennessee. I'm giving myself eleven more months to finish it, and then its back to work at the university."

"I heard you were attacked by a bear this week, dear. Are you doing okay now?" Mae asked.

"I'm fine. Luckily, Silas showed up and shot it. He probably saved my life."

"Oh my, it's a lucky thing he came along and had a gun with him," Mae said.

Tessa wondered if Mae didn't like Silas for more than just his brief stint in prison.

"Austin, what do you do for a living?" Martin asked.

"In the summer, I'm a fishing guide for one of the businesses in town. In the winter, I'm a hunting guide."

"I bet you've had some close calls with bears then."

"Yes, sir. A few, I guess. I try to keep my distance when I see one."

While the conversation continued, Silas leaned over and whispered to Tessa. "Why did you invite that woman?"

"Mae? I saw her at the store when I was buying supplies for the cookout, and she sort of invited herself. Why?"

Before he could answer, Mae interrupted. "Tessa, I sure see your Mr.

Newberry's truck here a lot since he finished with the shed."

"It's not completely finished yet, Mrs. Nicholson," Silas said.

"You must be doing your work at night then because that's when I mostly see you here," she replied.

"He's been helping me with some research at night about the mountains for my book," Tessa explained. She placed her hand on Silas' thigh, hoping he'd take the signal to not say anything else. She didn't want any discord today.

"Research, eh? Is that what they call it nowadays?" Mae replied.

Everyone laughed. Silas got up, walked over to the grill, and checked the knobs. Tessa felt her face getting warm, but laughed along with them. "I'll go get the dessert from the kitchen."

Sara followed her inside. "What was that all about?"

"I'm not sure, but Mae sure doesn't like Silas, and I don't want any problems between them today. Silas has been the perfect gentleman to her, and she continues to say terrible things about him."

"If she starts in on him again, I'll try to steer the conversation in a different direction," Sara said.

"Thanks. I'd really appreciate that. I don't know how much more he can take before saying something he shouldn't." She handed Sara some dessert plates, forks, and a gallon of ice cream, while she carried a cake.

When they walked back outside, Tessa saw Mae and Silas standing next to the cooler and having what looked like an intense conversation. Mae shook her head no and then turned and walked back to the table.

After finishing dessert, Silas, Martin, Sara, and Mae started playing cards and Austin helped Tessa take some of the food back into the kitchen.

"Thanks for helping," Tessa said.

"No problem. I don't really like playing cards," he said.

"How long have you known Silas?" she asked.

"A few years, I guess."

"How did you meet?"

"I don't really remember."

"You don't?" Apparently, he was keeping Silas' secrets as well.

"I really don't. It was probably at one of the bars in town."

The kitchen door opened and Silas walked in. "It's getting late, and we need to go," he said to Austin.

Tessa looked at her watch. "It's not that late."

"I have some work to do early in the morning."

"On a holiday?" she asked.

"It's an extra job I took on, and the owner wants to be home when I work there."

"I'll go get the grill ready to load back in the truck," Austin said.

"Thanks," Silas said.

Austin walked outside, leaving them alone in the kitchen.

Silas took her hands into his. "You threw a great party."

"Your burgers were really good."

Silas pulled her into his arms for a kiss. He captured her mouth with such a hungry urgency that it actually forced the breath from her lungs. "I've missed you," he whispered between kisses.

"Can you come back later and spend the night?"

"Don't tempt me, but I can't. Besides, you have Sara staying here. I don't think I could do my best work knowing she was in the next room, if you know what I mean." He winked and then kissed her again.

Suddenly, the kitchen door slammed and Silas and Tessa jumped apart. "I just wanted to tell you goodbye, dear," Mae said, walking over to the refrigerator to get the bowl of leftover watermelon.

Tessa glanced at Silas, who looked annoyed, and then back at Mae. "I'm glad you could come, Mae."

"I'll stop by next week, and we can talk," Mae said as she walked out the door.

"What does she want to talk about?"

"You, I guess." Tessa teased.

Quickly, Silas stole one more kiss. "I've got to go."

They walked back outside, and he helped Austin load the grill. Once they were finished, Silas gave her a peck on the cheek and then a wave as he and Austin drove off.

"I'm afraid we need to leave also," Elaine said with Martin standing behind her. "Can I help with any cleaning before I go?"

"Thanks, but there's not that much to do. Sara and I can handle it," Tessa said as Sara joined her.

"It was nice meeting you, Sara."

"You too. Thank you for coming."

Elaine grabbed Martin's hand, and they walk home together.

Tessa and Sara finish taking everything inside, making sure not to leave any food scraps outside that might attract bears. Inside, they put the last of the food in the refrigerator and washed the few dishes that needed it.

"I'm so glad I came down here this weekend," Sara said.

"Me too. I really needed to see you. I've been getting a little homesick."

"Really? Even with that hunky Silas around?"

"Yeah, even with him around. It's lonely with no girlfriend to talk to like we used to do."

"You know you can call me any time."

"You're such a great friend, Sara." She gave her friend a hug, and after finally getting everything cleaned and put away, they sat in the living room to talk. "I know you're leaving tomorrow, but I'm so tired. Would you mind if I went to bed instead of talking more?"

"No, not at all. I'm worn out too and flying home tomorrow is going to make for a long day," Sara said.

Both ladies said goodnight and headed to bed, but even after a hot shower, Tessa couldn't sleep. She just kept tossing and turning in bed. When her cell phone rang, she grabbed it. Blocked number. Silas, no doubt. "Hello," she said.

"Hello, sweetheart."

He had never called her that before and it gave her a warm feeling inside. "Hello."

"I couldn't sleep and hope I'm not interrupting you and Sara talking."

"We both turned in early, but I can't sleep, either."

"I had a really great time today."

"Me, too. I think it went well." She paused. "Silas, what were you and Mae talking about today?"

"Oh, it wasn't anything. She was telling me that I was taking advantage of you, and I told her you were a grown woman fully capable of making your own decisions. She didn't like my answer and walked away." He laughed. "I don't think she likes me very much."

"I think you're probably right. You know, Sara is leaving tomorrow morning, so if you want to stop by tomorrow night, I'll be here."

"I'd really like to, but I'm going to be busy for the next couple days. How about I take you out for dinner on Tuesday night? I know this special place that I would love to take you to."

"That sounds great."

"It's a date then. I'll call you Tuesday and let you know what time I'll pick you up. I better let you go now. Sweet dreams, beautiful lady."

"Goodnight, Silas." After hanging up the phone, Tessa had no problem falling asleep.

* * * * *

CHAPTER 4

SILAS got out of his truck and looked at the big pole barn in front of him. He took a deep breath, opened the door, and entered. The rear of the large room looked like a meat processing plant with lots of stainless steel equipment, but nearer to the door sat several men at some tables talking. A few of the men said hello to him, and then he saw a familiar face at a nearby table and joined him.

"Hey, Austin. I didn't think I'd see you here so soon," Silas said.

"Apparently, I made a good impression."

"Gentlemen, if I may have your attention," a familiar voice called out. Martin Pratt walked over to the tables, and the room fell quiet. "As you can see from the activity in the back, you all have done a very good job of finding bears this time. I already have buyers set up for the paws, claws, and skins. You'll find a little extra bonus money in your pay envelopes when you leave today." The men cheered and clapped upon hearing that. "Our next hunt is scheduled for next week in the Chattahoochee National Forest, and those of you that will be going, will be hunting elk. Now, I don't need to remind you that elk hunting in Georgia is illegal, but then most of the hunting we do is illegal, right?"

Martin and the men laughed, including Austin and Silas.

"This is what I came for," Austin said, smiling.

"You came to the right place then," Silas replied.

"Seriously, men, be careful out there and don't get caught. Lastly, I want to introduce you to a new hunter I just hired. Austin, stand up," Martin said.

Austin stood.

"This is Austin Drake. He's been a guide for one of the local hunting and fishing stores in town for about a year and is highly regarded by them. If they only knew I'm borrowing him from their legitimate business." More laughter and Austin sat back down. "All right, men, you can pick up your money in the office. Be back here on Monday and bring enough clothes for several nights."

The men stood up and followed Martin to the office to get their money. Silas got up to get a couple beers from the refrigerator by the door. He sat back down and handed one to Austin.

"Aren't you going to get your money?" Austin asked.

"It'll be there when I leave."

Two of the other men joined them at the table. "How's it goin', Silas?" one of the men asked as he thumbed through the money in his envelope.

"Pretty good, Greg. How's things with you?'

"Not bad."

"Greg, this is Austin Drake. Austin, Greg Rollins."

Austin and Greg shook hands. "Welcome to the club," Greg said, taking a swig of beer.

"Thanks. I'm looking forward to some of that bonus money, you got there."

"It's definitely good money. Silas, I'm having some trouble sightin' in my new rifle. Think you could take a look at it?" Greg asked.

"Sure."

"You think you'll have time?" another man asked as he walked up.

"Austin, this is Mac Conrad."

Austin nodded to Mac.

"Now, why wouldn't I have time, Mac?"

"Well, I hear tell you been keeping busy with a pretty new gal in town."

"How do you know that?" Silas asked. Under the table, his hands curled into fists.

"As I understand it, you're at Martin's neighbor's house all the time, and his wife saw you going out to your truck the other night naked as a jaybird. Sounds to me like she must be a good fuck."

Silas' rage quickly reached the breaking point. He leaped across the table, taking Mac down to the floor. Both started punching each other, but with Silas on top, he made the better hits.

Austin pulled Silas off, and Greg pulled Mac away. Both men tried to wrestle out of their grasp. Martin came out of his office and ran over. "What the hell is going on?"

"Nothing. It's over," Silas said, rubbing his knuckles while staring down Mac.

"Yeah, it's done." Mac wiped the blood from his lip and walked away, followed by Greg.

Silas picked up his chair and sat back down at the table with Austin. Martin joined them.

"You need to control that temper, son."

"He said something about Tessa I didn't like." Silas, still angry at Mac's comments, knew Martin was the only person who could have told him.

"I'll handle Mac. Right now, I've got a job for you." Martin pulled out a map from his pocket and put it on the table. "I've got two clients coming in at the end of the week for an elk hunt. I need for you two to go bait the area this week. Silas, on Friday morning I want you to take them out for the hunt." He unfolded the map. "Here is where I need the bait placed." He pointed to an area just outside of the park in North Carolina. "It's far enough away from any of the ranger stations that you should be okay, but keep an eye out anyway. These hunters are rich and could easily be repeat customers for future hunts."

Silas looked over the map. "Yes, sir, we'll get the bait out."

Martin handed Silas an envelope and got up from the table. "I think you'll be happy with Friday's hunt, son." He slapped him on the shoulder as he walked away.

Silas opened the envelope filled with the payment for his last job. "I've got to go. I'm taking Tessa out to dinner tonight."

He and Austin got up and walked out to their trucks. At Silas' truck, Austin stopped. "I know it's none of my business, but after what happened in there, do you think it's a good idea to have a relationship with Tessa? She's a nice lady, and I'd hate to see her get hurt."

"You're right. It's none of your business. I know what I'm doing. Besides, in a year, she'll be heading back to her old job up north."

"A lot can happen in a year."

"Don't worry about it. I've got it under control." Silas got in his truck and spun dirt as he drove away.

* * *

LATER that evening, Silas knocked on Tessa's door to take her to dinner. She looked beautiful when the door opened. Dressed in a green sweater and tight jeans, she also wore heeled shoes that made her about two-inches taller. Almost as tall as him.

"You look great." He gave her a kiss on the cheek. "Are you ready to go?"

"I am." She picked up her sweater and walked with him out the door.

He helped her into his truck and then they drove off toward the National Park.

"Where are we going?"

"Over the mountains into North Carolina to my favorite restaurant."

Halfway across the mountains, Silas pulled off the road at one of the overlooks in the Park.

"Why are we stopping?"

"I thought we'd watch the sun set over the mountains." They got out and leaned on the front of the truck. Silas reached over and captured her hand.

As the sun sat behind the mountains, it looked as though orange-colored rays were sprouting out from the top of them.

"It's so beautiful," she said.

"Just like you." He turned and kissed her. Out of the corner of his eye, he saw something move. "Look."

Walking out from the trees in the meadow below them were two young deer.

"They're so pretty, aren't they?"

"Yeah, they are." He thought about the hunt he was guiding at the end of the week and how one of the hunter's would love to have just one of those deer in his sights. Suddenly, a feeling of guilt swept over him. "We better go."

Back on the road, it didn't take long for them to reach North Carolina and Joe's BBQ and Tavern. Silas held the truck door open and took her hand as she got out. "Joe has the best barbecue ribs around, and he makes his own secret sauce. You'll love it."

He opened the door of the restaurant, and they walked inside to the large bar area. The lights were dimmed and country music blared from the speakers in the corners of the room. Silas led her to a table in the back of the bar. There were several available tables closer to the front of the business, but he didn't want a lot of distractions during their date. The waitress came over, and Silas order them both a beer.

"Joe's Special Baby Back ribs are his best."

"That sounds really good. I love barbecue ribs," Tessa said.

The waitress brought the beers, and Silas ordered. "Bring us both a platter of Joe's Special Baby Back Ribs."

"Thanks, sweetie," the waitress said, winking at Silas and headed to the kitchen with the order.

"How did you find this place?'

"I used to come here for lunch every day when I hunted in this area." As soon as the words left his mouth, he regretted it.

"You hunted every day around here?"

"Did I say hunted? I meant I used to eat here when I worked some construction in the area."

"I see."

After they had finished their food, a tall, dark man approached the table. Silas immediately stood and shook his hand. "Joe, how ya doing, man."

"I'm great." He pulled Silas into a quick hug. "It's good to see you. I thought maybe the law had caught up with you."

Silas ignored the statement. "Joe, this is my friend Tessa. She's living over the mountain in Yellowwood. I told her she had to have some of the best ribs in the Blue Ridge Mountains."

Joe laughed. "Hello, Tessa. I hope you enjoyed the ribs."

"Oh my yes, they were excellent. Silas was right when he said you have the best barbecue around."

"I'm glad to hear it. She's a beautiful woman, Silas. You better take good care of her."

"I plan on it."

"Don't be a stranger around here and bring this lucky lady back soon."

"I will. Thanks."

Joe walked away and just as Silas sat back down, Mac and Greg walked in and took a seat at the bar. "We need to go." He threw some money on the table and got up.

"Right now?"

"Yes, right now and let's go out through the family room."

"Why?"

"Let's just go."

He quickly ushered Tessa through the family room and outside to the parking lot. He clicked his remote to unlock the truck doors and just as he did, he heard Mac call out his name.

"Hey, Silas. Is that your little lady?"

He looked at Tessa. "Get in the truck and lock the door. No matter what, don't get out." He handed her the keys.

Silas turned to see both Mac and Greg walking toward them.

Before Tessa could get into the truck, Mac shouted to her. "Hey pretty lady, did Silas tell you about his shady past?"

"He's drunk. Get in the truck," Silas told her and turned back to the men. "You need to take Mac home, Greg. He's had too much to drink tonight."

"Oh, come on, man. I want to meet your woman, Silas." Mac continued walking toward them.

Tessa climbed into the truck and shut the door. Silas stepped in front of Mac to block his way just as Mac took a swing at him. Silas blocked the punch and hit Mac in the stomach. He doubled over and fell to the ground.

"Take him home, Greg." Silas got into his truck and drove off.

Tessa didn't say a word as they pulled out onto the road.

"I'm sorry about that," he said.

"Who was that guy?"

"Just a guy I know. He likes to drink, and he'd had a little much tonight. He's a real jerk, and I didn't want him around you."

After that, other than the country music on the radio, the drive back to Tessa's was in complete silence. Tessa did slide over on the seat next to Silas, who then put his arm around her as she laid her head on his shoulder.

When they arrived at her house, Silas turned off the truck, but left the radio on. They just sat in the dark and listened to the music until he finally broke the silence. "I'm sorry about tonight. I really wanted it to be a special night. I didn't intend on it ending with me punching a guy in the parking lot."

Tessa sat up straight. "I know about your past," she blurted out.

Shocked, Silas couldn't speak. He just sat there trying to figure out how to explain.

Before he could respond, she continued. "I paid for one of those Internet background checks and found your criminal history."

"I don't know what to say."

"You don't need to say anything. I'm okay with your past, but I have a couple questions."

"Yeah, what's that?"

"If you were convicted of a felony, how can you carry a gun?"

"I actually can't."

"You told me you always carry one."

"I do a lot of work in secluded locations around here. It's more for self-protection from animals than anything else."

"I don't think the police would see it that way."

"No, probably not. What's your other question?"

"Are you mad at me for checking into your background?"

"No, I'm not mad. A little embarrassed maybe, but not mad." A little ashamed though, he thought to himself. "Maybe I should explain."

"No, you don't need to."

She moved closer and kissed him. She laid her hand on his chest and slowly moved it downward. He felt himself becoming hard as she probed her tongue deep into his mouth. He grabbed her roaming hand before she reached the bulging erection inside his tight jeans.

"Stay with me tonight," she whispered.

His body told him yes, but his head told him no. "I want to, I really do, but I can't tonight. I have to be up early for work, and if I stayed tonight, I'd never make it to work in the morning. I'm sorry."

He turned the key to shut the power off to the radio and got out of the truck. He walked around to help her out. His throbbing shaft made walking a little uncomfortable.

They stopped at her kitchen door, and she kissed him again, asking once more. "We could set the alarm so you wouldn't be late in the morning."

"You have no idea how much I want to stay. I promise I'll stay this weekend. That is, if you still want me to."

"Of course, I want you to."

He was happy to hear that. He looked deep into her eyes and brushed a few wisps of hair away from her face. Once more he kissed her before unlocking the door for her to go inside. "I'm going to be pretty busy all week and may even have to go out of town for a job, but I'll call you before Saturday."

"Okay."

"Make sure you lock the door as soon as I leave."

"I will. Be careful working this week."

"Always." He smiled and gave her one more quick kiss before going back to his truck and leaving. Silas didn't go home though. Instead, he drove straight to Mac's house, an old shack at the end of a dead end road high on a mountain. The closer he drove to Mac's, the angrier he got. In his mind, Mac had no business trying to get to Tessa.

When he drove up to Mac's house, he knew the man was home when he saw his truck parked out front. He shut the truck off, but left the headlights shining at the front door. When Silas approached the cabin, Mac came out carrying a shotgun.

"Who the fuck is out here?" he shouted, using his hand to try and to block out the blinding light from Silas' truck.

Silas was close enough to grab the shotgun and whip Mac in the face with the butt. Mac fell to the ground groaning and holding his nose. Silas unloaded the shells from the gun and tossed it to the ground, throwing the shells out into the yard. He pulled Mac up by his shirt collar. "If you ever come near Tessa again, I'll kill you. Do you understand?"

"I understand."

He let go, and Mac dropped to the ground. Silas walked back into his truck and left.

* * *

BEFORE daylight on Friday morning, Silas arrived at Martin's barn to meet the hunters he was taking on the elk hunt. Martin hadn't told him much about them except they were from Nebraska and had mostly hunted small game animals. They each wanted an elk head to mount on their walls.

Silas, dressed in camouflaged overalls with a T-shirt underneath, wore a bandana around his head to hold the hair out of his eyes. He opened the door to the barn and entered the brightly lit building. It took a moment for his eyes to adjust to the light before he saw Martin sitting at the table. He walked over and sat down.

"Where are the hunters?"

Martin nodded over toward the bathroom.

"They're in there."

"Together?"

Just then, the bathroom door opened and out walked two women dressed in hunting clothes.

"You've got to be kidding," Silas said.

"Just remember, they're paying big money for this hunt," Martin said as he stood. "Ladies, this is Silas, your guide for the hunt. Silas, this is Ginger and Barbara."

"Good morning, ladies."

"Oh, this is going to be fun," Ginger, the redhead, said, looking up and down Silas' body.

"If you're ready, we probably should get going so we can be in place when the sun comes up."

The ladies agreed, and Silas led them outside to his truck. He stowed their gear under the backseat and opened the passenger door for them. Ginger got in first and scooted to the middle. Barbara got in after her. Silas got in on the driver's side and started the truck. He drove away from the barn and out onto the road.

"What kind of hunting experience do you ladies have?"

"We grew up on a farm and our daddy took us squirrel and rabbit hunting. I'm pretty sure he wanted sons," Barbara said.

"When we popped out, he taught us how to hunt instead," Ginger added.

"Oh, you're sisters."

"Yes. Deer are about the biggest animals we've hunted, and we wanted to try something bigger," Ginger said, placing her hand on Silas' thigh.

Without even taking his eyes off the road, he gently moved her hand away. "Well, with any luck you'll be able to get an elk today."

"That's what we're hoping for," Barbara said.

They arrived at their destination before sunrise. It was the same spot he and Austin had been baiting all week, so he was pretty sure they would at least see some elk. Shooting the animals would be up to the ladies' skill.

Silas got the guns out and gave them to the ladies. Once loaded, they were ready. "We need to be very quiet. Elk have amazing hearing and can be spooked with the slightest sound."

"Where are we going?" Barbara asked.

"We'll follow that trail to the top of the hill." He pointed to a narrow trail to the right of the truck. "On the other side is a meadow where they like to graze in the mornings."

"This is so exciting," Ginger said, moving over closer to Silas.

The three of them hiked up the hill in silence and took their place on the ground with their guns resting on a log, aimed toward the meadow below. It was a waiting game now. As soon as the sun rose, a small herd of elk stepped out from the trees and began grazing.

"If you both want to take an animal, you'll have to shoot at the same time. Once they hear a shot, they'll take off," Silas whispered.

"I want the big one on the left," Ginger whispered back.

"I'll take the one on the right," Barbara replied.

Both ladies did a countdown and then shot. Each hit their target animal, and the rest of the herd scattered quickly.

"Whoo-whoo. We did it!" Barbara shouted, jumping up and doing a little dance.

"First shot! Damn, that was nice." Ginger skipped over to Silas giving him a hug and a kiss.

She surprised him, but he attributed it to her excitement of hitting her target. "Nice shots, ladies. From the look of it, I doubt they ran very far. You go down and see if you can find them. I'll bring the truck around the side of the hill and into the meadow to load them," Silas said.

The ladies took off down the hill to find their prizes, and Silas walked back to the truck. Before he drove down to meet them, he took a small notepad out of the glove compartment and scribbled something down on it before tossing it back inside. When he drove the truck into the meadow, the girls were waiting for him.

"They both dropped a few feet inside the tree line," Barbara told him.

He pulled the truck over where they showed him and got out. "Unload your guns and stow them in the back under the seat and I'll drag the animals over."

He used the winch on the front of his truck to drag the animals closer and with the lift on the back of his truck, he got them loaded in the bed. He covered the carcasses with a couple of tarps. "Get in, ladies. We need to get out of here in case anyone heard your shots."

The girls jumped in the truck, seating arrangement the same as when they had arrived.

"I'm so excited to have gotten one on my first shot," Barbara said.

"Me, too. John will be so proud of you," Ginger said.

"Is that your husband?" Silas asked.

"Yes, John's her husband, but I'm not married," Ginger gave him a wink and scooted a little closer to Silas.

He had a feeling this conversation was heading in the wrong direction and needed to change the topic. "You said you wanted to mount the heads. Will you also want the meat too? We can do all of the processing no matter how you want them, but Martin will need to know when we get back to the barn."

"We want the meat butchered and packaged for eating and the heads mounted," Barbara said.

"That won't be a problem. It can all be shipped around the same time, as long as you have paid in advance."

"Money is no object with us. We are very well off," Ginger said, running her fingertip up and down the inside of Silas' thigh. He nearly ran the truck off the road.

When they arrived at the barn, Silas drove the truck around to the back of the building and pulled out his cell phone to activate the garage door to open. He drove inside where several men approached the truck and started unloading the animals.

"They want the heads mounted and the meat wrapped for shipping to them," Silas instructed.

Martin walked up and greeted them. "It looks like you had a productive day."

"Oh, it was wonderful, Mr. Pratt," Barbara said.

"Yes and thank you so much for letting Silas take us on the hunt. He was wonderful," Ginger said, smiling at Silas.

"Come with me, ladies. Let's go to a less messy area of the building." He led them over to the front of the barn where they had been that morning. Silas followed.

"We want to celebrate tonight. Where's a good place to get some food and drinks in town?" Ginger asked,

"The Black Bear Bar and Restaurant is a good place, and it's only a couple blocks from your hotel. They have great food and drinks," Martin said.

"That sounds perfect." Ginger turned to Silas. "You will join us, won't you, Silas?" She walked her fingers over his chest.

"I actually have plans tonight." He grabbed her hand, pushing it away.

"Sorry, but I don't think I can make it."

Both Ginger and Barbara looked disappointed, especially Ginger who pouted with her lower lip stuck out.

"I need to go to the restroom. Come on, Ginger," Barbara said. The ladies walked away from the two men. Ginger kept her eyes on Silas as she walked past, still pouting.

After the ladies left, Martin turned to Silas. "What do you mean you have plans? These are paying customers, and I want to keep them happy so they'll be returning. If they want you to party with them, you'll party with them. Got it?" He shoved a brown envelope into Silas chest. "Here's your payment for today."

A few minutes later the girls walked back out.

"Change of plans, ladies. Silas said he'll meet you at the Black Bear Bar tonight at seven," Martin said.

The ladies cheered, especially Ginger, who looked at Silas while running her tongue over her lips. Silas knew he would be in trouble partying with this girl and probably in even more trouble after promising Tessa he would be there tonight. "Sure, seven o'clock. I'll see you then." He turned and left the barn.

Dammit. He really wanted to spend the evening with Tessa and make good on his promise to spend the weekend with her, but Martin paid him good money for his work. The job had to come first. He'd have to call and make something up. Pulling out his phone, he dialed Tessa's number.

The phone rang a few times, and he almost wished it would go to her voicemail, rather than have to speak to her to break their date, but he wasn't that lucky. "Hello."

"Hi, Tessa. It's Silas."

"I'm so glad you called. I thought I'd order a pizza tonight, if that's okay with you. That way we can spend the whole night here."

"I'm sorry, but I can't make it tonight."

"What?"

"Something came up with a job I'm working on, and I have to go pick up a shipment of ceramic tiles in Knoxville tonight. I'll probably just spend the night there and bring it all back in the morning. I promise I'll make it up to you tomorrow night."

"What if I came with you? I'd love to see Knoxville," she suggested.

"No, no, that won't work. I have to pick up the shipment late at the airport, and I'll probably just sleep in my truck."

"Well, okay. I guess I'll see you tomorrow night then."

"I promise. Thanks for understanding. Bye."

He ended the call abruptly. He could hear the disappointment in her voice and hated lying to her. He seemed to be doing a lot of that lately.

* * *

THAT night, at seven o'clock on the dot, Silas walked into the Black Bear Bar. He didn't think the ladies seemed like the family room type, so he entered through bar side and immediately knew they were there and had already started their celebration.

"Oh Si-las. We're over here, Silas."

He walked the end of the bar where they sat, and Ginger jumped over to the next stool so he would have to sit between them. Both ladies moved their stools closer to him. He felt like he was the meat inside a sandwich. He probably was. It appeared they had been there drinking for a while.

The bartender came over to Silas. "I'll take a beer."

"Put it on our tab," Barbara said. "And, bring us both another margarita."

"Have you two eaten anything yet?" Silas asked.

Barbara thought for a second. "No, I don't think we have."

"The only thing I want to eat is you," Ginger said, putting her hand on his inner thigh.

"Maybe we better get some food into both of you," he said, removing her hand.

"The bartender brought their drinks and sat them down on the bar.

"Could you bring the ladies each a basket of wings?" Silas asked.

"Oh, oh, I want some breadsticks too," Ginger said.

The bartender looked at Silas, who nodded. The ladies started drinking their margaritas, but Silas only sipped on his beer. He feared he had a long night ahead of him.

"You know, you're really cute, Silas," Ginger said, putting her arm over his shoulder and tickling his ear.

"I've been told that a few times."

"Don't you think we're cute too?" Barbara asked, putting her arm around his shoulder.

"Ah, yeah, sure. I thought you ladies were married."

"She's the married one. I'm the wild single one." Ginger took another drink of her margarita.

"That's never stopped me before," Barbara said. "Are you married, Silas?"

"No."

"Oh, goodie," Ginger said.

The bartender brought their chicken wings and breadsticks with some cheese.

"Oh my God, I'm starved," Barbara said. She picked up a chicken wing and started eating.

"Me, too." Ginger picked up one of the breadsticks and dipped it into the cheese. "Silas, don't you wish this were you?" She took most of the breadstick in her mouth and slid it out, sucking off the cheese.

Uncomfortable, he shifted a little on his stool.

"You know, our hotel is only a couple blocks from here. We could go back there and continue our party in private," she suggested.

Barbara again moved a little closer to him. "Have you ever had a threesome?"

He nearly choked on his beer.

Before he could respond, he heard a voice behind him. "Yes, Silas. Have you ever had a threesome?"

He turned to find Tessa standing behind him. Arms crossed in front of her, she did not look happy. Her neighbor, Mae stood behind her.

The ladies looked at Tessa. "We've never done a foursome before, but I think there's enough of Silas to go around, if you want to come," Ginger said.

Silas thought he actually saw Tessa change to a deep shade of red. She turned and ran out of the bar.

"Shame on you," Mae said before following after her.

"Tessa, wait." Silas threw some money on the bar and tried to chase after her, but the two ladies held onto to him to hold him back. By the time he had broken free, Tessa and Mae had already reached her car. He ran up to the door. "Tessa, let me explain," he pleaded as she backed her car out of the parking spot.

She wouldn't look at him as she shifted into drive and pulled away. He quickly started toward his truck, but found the two drunk women standing next to it.

"She left?"

"Yes, she left."

"That's too bad, but we can still have some fun, right?" Ginger asked.

"No, we cannot still have some fun!" He was furious.

"Come on, Silas. Wouldn't you rather be with us instead of her?" Barbara said.

"No."

Disappointed, they got the point and went back into the bar. Silas looked down the road Tessa had left on. "Damn it!" His fist came down hard on the hood of his truck.

* * * * *

CHAPTER 5

AS soon as Mae got in the car, Tessa locked the doors, threw the car into reverse, and backed out of the parking spot. Silas had caught up to them and was pleading for her to stop, but she didn't. She didn't want to talk to him. Shifting into drive, she sped out onto the street, leaving him in the parking lot with those sluts that had followed him out.

"Tessa, I'm so sorry. This is entirely my fault. I should have never suggested that we go to dinner there," Mae said.

"It's no one's fault. You didn't know he would be there. He wasn't even supposed to be in town. I can't believe he lied to me. Out of town, he said." She wiped the tears from her eyes.

"Honey, he's no good. You need to forget him. You know, I know someone who would be perfect for you."

"Thanks, Mae, but I don't think I want to go out with another man for a long time."

"Well, if you change your mind."

Tessa drove up the hill toward their neighborhood and then turned the car into Mae's driveway. "Thanks for dinner and for backing me up. I don't think I could have handled that scene with Silas alone."

Mae patted Tessa's hand. "You call me anytime you need to talk, dear." She got out of the car, and Tessa waited until the elder lady made it safely inside the house before she backed out and went home.

Just as she turned off the car, her cell phone rang. It showed a blocked number. She rejected the call, and went inside, straight to the refrigerator to get a bottle of wine. Her phone rang again, and again she rejected it. This time she turned it off.

She took the bottle of wine and a glass to the living room and sat on the couch. As she poured the wine, she thought about how she had planned on sharing that bottle with Silas tonight. "Well, it's all mine now." She drank almost the whole glass in one drink. After several more glasses, she lay down on the couch and cried herself to sleep.

Tessa was startled awake when she heard banging at the kitchen door. The clock on the wall showed midnight, and then she heard someone shouting her name. She recognized the voice. Afraid that the pounding and shouting would wake the neighbors, she went to the door and flung it open. "Will you stop that!"

"Tessa, please let me explain."

"I don't want to see you. Please go away." She started to close the door.

"Wait! I'm not leaving until you let me explain. I'll stay here pounding on your door all night, if I have to."

"Silas, it's not just what happened tonight. It's the lying and all the secrets."

"The secrets are for your protection, I swear."

"I know you're still into something illegal, something with the Pratts. I don't understand why you would still be involved in something like that, but that's your business. I don't think we should see each other anymore." She did her best to keep the tears from flowing, but was losing the battle.

He was silent for what seemed like forever and when she started to close the door again he finally spoke up. "Wait. If that's what you want, fine, but you're wrong about me. You just won't listen." He turned and went back to his truck.

She closed the door and after hearing his truck start and drive away from the house, she went to bed crying.

* * *

TESSA slept late the next morning, then around noon Mae stopped by. "Please come in, Mae."

"I brought you some cookies and wanted to apologize again for suggesting dinner at that bar last night. Are you feeling better today?"

"Thanks. You have nothing to apologize for, and I'm not sure how I feel yet. Silas came to see me last night, and I ended things with him. Now, when I think about it, maybe I should have let him explain before breaking it off with him."

"No, I think you were right to end it. You don't need to be involved with someone like him."

"I thought maybe he had changed from the person who committed those crimes to someone—well, someone different. I guess I was wrong."

They sat in silence for a few moments.

"Mae, if you wouldn't mind, I think I'd like to be alone. I want to work on my book today and hopefully that will take my mind off of what happened."

"Of course, honey. If you need anything, you call me now, you hear?"

"I will and thank you for the cookies."

Mae left and Tessa went to her computer and began typing. Before she knew it, she was *in the zone* and had finished another chapter. Looking at the clock, she realized she had worked straight through lunch and walked to the kitchen to get a bite to eat. She noticed her phone sitting on the table. She forgot she had turned it off last night and picked it up to turn it on. Once it had synced, the voicemail beeped. She checked and found seven messages. She knew they were probably all from Silas and was tempted not listen, but decided to dial the voicemail number and see what he had to say.

All seven messages asked for forgiveness, saying what she saw at the bar was not what it seemed to be, and that he could explain if given the chance. She deleted each message and hung up the phone. It didn't make her feel better or give her any idea what to do. Maybe she should give him a chance to explain?

She heard a knock at the cabin's front door. Since coming to Yellowwood, no one had ever used her front door. She went to the door and looked through the window to find a flower deliveryman standing there holding a vase of red roses. She opened the door.

"I have a delivery for Tessa Cooper."

"I'm Tessa Cooper."

"I guess these are for you then." He handed her the roses.

She took them, and the deliveryman turned to leave. "Wait, let me get you a tip."

"No need. The tip was already taken care of by the sender. Have a nice day, ma'am."

"Thank you."

She took the flowers to the kitchen and sat them on the table, removing the card from the holder. She counted each flower. Twelve red roses and they were beautiful. She leaned in to take a whiff of their sweet scent and opened the card. Of course, they were from Silas. Like his phone messages, said he was sorry and asked for another chance. At that moment, her cell phone rang. The caller ID showed a blocked number.

"Hello."

"Tessa, please don't hang up. It's Silas."

"I know." She sat down at the table.

"I left you about a dozen messages last night."

"It was seven, and I listened to them this morning. I turned my phone off last night after your first two calls."

"I'm so sorry about what you saw last night. If you will just give me a chance to explain, I think you'll understand. Afterward, if you still don't want see me, I'll leave you alone."

"I got your flowers."

"I hope you liked them."

"I do. They're beautiful."

"Have dinner with me, at my house?"

"I don't know, Silas."

"I'll explain everything, and I'll answer any questions you have. Please."

She did want answers, this might be the only way to get them, and he had made the gesture of offering to take her to his home. At least that would no longer be a secret, and if he meant what he said about answering all of her questions, the least she could do was hear him out since that's what she had wanted all along. "Okay. One dinner at your house, and that's all."

"Thank you."

"Give me directions so I can find you."

"I'll need to pick you up."

"Why?" She felt the hair on her neck stand up. Another stall?

"My place is really hard to find. You'd never find it with directions, and there's one other thing."

"What's that?"

"The dinner will have to be next Friday."

"Friday? That's a week away. Why?" she asked.

"I'm going out of town today for work and won't be back until Friday, but I swear that's the truth. I really am going out of town."

She wondered if he were going to meet those women again. Even though the thought of him being with another woman infuriated her, she had no hold over him. He could do whatever with whomever he wanted, but she was curious about his secrets and wanted answers. "Okay, next Friday."

"Great. I'll call you when I get back in town. Thank you, Tessa."

"Goodbye, Silas." She ended the call. She was glad she was going to have dinner with him, but she was still skeptical.

* * *

MARTIN Pratt sat in his office in the barn with Mac and Greg across the desk from him when Silas walked through the door.

"You wanted to see me?"

"Gentlemen, will you leave Silas and me alone?" That was more an order than a request. The two men left the room and closed the door behind them. "Sit down."

Silas sat in the seat vacated by Mac. "Look, I'm sorry about what happened last night."

"You're sorry? You're sorry! Do you have any idea how much money those women paid me for that little hunt you took them on? Thousands and they were not happy when I talked to them this morning. They told me you weren't very accommodating to them. I'll be surprised if they ever come back for another hunt. I had to give their money back just to appease them and hopefully not lose them as customers. You cost me a lot of money with that stunt last night."

"They were drunk and wanted to have sex. I was hired to be a guide, not to be pimped out."

"Anyone else would have leaped at the chance to have sex with two beautiful women like that."

"Then next time, find someone else." Silas stood.

Martin leaned forward, and pointed his finger at Silas. "You need to think about whether you want to remain working for me or not. I'm the boss. When I tell you to do something I expect it to be done, and I expect the customer to be happy afterward. Understand?"

"Yes. I need to get on the road for that delivery. Do you have the keys to the truck?"

Martin took a set of keys out of the drawer and tossed them to Silas. He handed him a brown envelope next. "That's the money you'll need for fuel, food, and lodging. There better not be any problems with this delivery."

Silas looked inside the envelope to count the money. "There won't be any problems. I'll be back at the end of the week."

He turned and left the office. Martin followed him out and watched until he left the building.

Mac and Greg sat at the table near the door. Martin joined them.

"He's become a real pain in the ass since he took up with that bitch across the street from you," Greg said.

"Yeah, but he's good at what he does, and he's never turned down a job yet."

"Until last night when he wouldn't fuck those women. If that would've been me, they still wouldn't be walking right," Mac said, laughing.

"If that would've been you, they wouldn't have wanted to fuck," Greg said.

"Yeah, well he didn't finish the job last night, and I think he needs to be taught a lesson."

"Calm down," Martin said. "I agree that Mr. Newberry needs to be taken down a notch or two, but let me think about how to do it."

"Let me do it, boss."

Mac seemed a little too eager to do the job, Martin thought, but was intrigued. "What do you have in mind?"

Mac perked up like the only rooster in the hen house. "When he comes back from his delivery, I can take him out in one shot as he's driving in on the parkway."

"That's an interesting idea, but a little drastic, don't you think?"

"Silas has been a pain in everyone's ass since he started with us," Greg pointed out. "No one would be sorry to see something happen to him."

"He's a loner and not a team player. He doesn't want to work with anyone, and none of us want to work with him," Mac said.

"That's why he's doing this delivery. He needs some time to think, away from that woman."

"Where's he going?" Greg asked.

"He's delivering some bear skins and claws to a distributor in Denver."

"Like I said, I can take care of him with one shot on the parkway," Mac pointed out again.

"I'm not sure that's a good idea. It's one thing to have the rangers after us for poaching, but it's another problem to be involved with a murder when he's driving one of my trucks."

Mac was one crazy son of a bitch, but Martin knew he would do whatever he asked of him. "We need to send him a message, but I don't want anyone hurt in the process, at least not yet."

"I have just the plan." Mac leered at the door that Silas just walked through.

* * *

TESSA didn't think Friday would ever arrive. Silas hadn't called at all and it worried her a little. She walked outside to get the newspaper and found the October morning cool and crisp. The autumn colors were at their peak. The reds, oranges, and yellows looked like a variegated blanket spread across the mountains.

Elaine Pratt was on her porch feeding her cat.

"Hello, Elaine."

"Good morning." She walked out to the mailbox. "How are you? I've barely seen you this week."

"I've been keeping busy inside."

"Have you had coffee yet? Martin is gone, and I just put a pot on. I think I have some coffee cake too. Please come in and join me."

"That sounds nice. Thanks."

The two ladies walked inside Elaine's home and into the kitchen. "Sit down and I'll get the coffee," Elaine said.

Tessa sat at the table while Elaine poured their coffee and brought cake with two plates and forks to the table.

"How's Silas? I haven't seen his truck over there at all this week."

"He's working out of town, but is supposed to be home tonight." She took a bite of the cake.

"You don't seem too excited about that. Is something wrong?"

"Last week, he told me that he was working out of town, but I caught him with two women at a bar in town. We had a fight. When he gets back tonight, we're supposed to talk things out."

"Listen, honey, I've seen him around you, and if he's not head over heels over you, then something's wrong," Elaine said.

"You think?"

"I do. Listen to what he has to say. Maybe the thing with those women might not have been what you thought. Don't rush into something unless you're sure."

Tessa took a sip of coffee and thought that was good advice, but didn't want to talk about it anymore and changed the subject. "When is he supposed to start working on your house? It was to add a room, right?"

"Yes, to add a room. I think Martin said something about waiting until spring now, when the weather is better."

"Where is Martin? You said he was out of town."

"He's gone to some hunting and fishing show in Knoxville. To tell you the truth, I kind of enjoy it when he's gone. I like the alone time." Both ladies laughed.

"I really should get back to the house. I have a lot of things to do today. Thanks for the coffee and cake."

"You barely touched either one."

"I'm sorry. I guess I have a lot on my mind." She got up and headed back to her cabin.

Inside, she started filling the sink with water to do the dishes. She couldn't help but think about what Elaine said about Silas caring so much for her. She was so angry with him, angry about the lies, angry about his secrets, and angry he's involved in some bad things, but had to admit to herself she'd had fallen in love with him.

She reached into the dishwater for another item to wash and grabbed the blade of a sharp knife, cutting herself. "Ouch!" It looked like a bad cut, and she decided she'd go to the clinic to get it checked out. She wrapped it in a clean towel, picked up her purse and keys, and drove to town.

At the clinic, she received four stitches and a prescription for an antibiotic. The pharmacy was a block down the street, and she walked to get the prescription filled. After leaving the pharmacy, she headed back up the street to car when she saw Austin walking toward her on the sidewalk. "Hi, Austin. How are you?"

"Hello, Tessa. It's good to see you. How is your book coming?"

"It's a slow process, especially when I have my mind on other things."

"Silas?"

"Yeah, we had a fight."

"He told me."

"Have you seen him?" she asked before realizing she shouldn't.

"No, he's been out of town this week doing some work."

"That's what he told me. Would you like to get a cup of coffee? I'd like to talk to you about him."

Austin looked at his watch. "I suppose I have time for a quick cup."

They walked next door to the coffee shop. It was busy, but they received their coffees quickly and sat down.

"How long have you known Silas?" she asked.

"I guess about three years now."

"Do you know about his criminal record?"

"Do you?"

"Yes. I paid for one of those online background checks after I met him, and then he told me about it." She lowered her head. "He's still involved in it, isn't he?"

Austin took a deep breath. "Tessa, I really like you, and Silas is my best friend. I'm going to be as honest as I can because you need to know what you're getting into. Yes, he's still poaching animals, and if you stay involved with him, you'll eventually get hurt."

"Is what he does dangerous?"

"It can be, but Silas is good, and he's careful."

"Are you part of it too?"

"I'd rather not talk about me. Look, you seem really nice and maybe it would be best for both you and Silas if you forget about him, at least until things settle down."

That answer pretty much meant that Austin was working for Martin too. "What do you mean, until things settle down? Is he in some kind of trouble?"

"I can't go into it. I've said too much already."

She let out a frustrating breath. Austin was keeping secrets too, and her hand was beginning to ache. "I suppose I should be getting home. Silas said we would talk tonight, and I have some things to do before he gets there. I don't want to keep you any longer."

Austin looked at his watch. "I think I'm going to stick around for just a little longer. I see a pretty little thing over there that I'd like to say hi to."

Tessa looked behind her and saw a cute blonde smiling at Austin. "Good luck and thanks for the talk."

Tessa left the coffee shop and started down the sidewalk toward her car. She felt more confused than ever. It seemed as though everyone likes Silas and likes her, but no one likes them together. It was getting late in the morning, and her hand was beginning to throb. She needed to get home to get ready for her date. She wasn't paying attention where she was walking and nearly ran right into a man on the sidewalk. "Excuse me. I'm so sorry." She looked up and realized that it was Mac Conrad, the man that Silas had fought with that night in the parking lot.

"Well, hello there little lady. How are you today?" He towered over her in both height and weight and had a bit of an odor about him that turned her stomach.

"I'm fine. If you'll excuse me." She tried to step around him, but he took a step to the left and blocked her way.

"You're Silas' woman, aren't you?"

Tessa needed to get away from this man. She was fearful of what he might do. "Yes, he's my friend. Please, I really need to be going."

"What's your hurry?" He grabbed her bandaged hand, and she winced in pain.

He leaned down into her face. "If you know what's good for your boyfriend, you'll tell him he needs to mind his own business and just do what the boss tells him."

"Tessa, is everything alright?" Austin walked up behind her, and Mac let go of her hand.

"Yes, everything is fine," she said, holding her bandaged hand.

"Mac, are you bothering Tessa, because I'd hate to see what Silas would do if he thought you were messing with her." Austin stepped between Mac and Tessa.

"This is Tessa? Silas' woman? Well, how about that. It's nice to meet you, ma'am." He tipped his ball cap to her.

Tessa took a step closer to Austin, trying to hide behind him.

"I was just on the way to my truck." Mac stepped around them and headed down the sidewalk. "Have a nice day."

Austin turned to Tessa. "Are you okay?"

"I'm fine. Thanks for your help. If you hadn't come by, I don't know how I would have gotten away from him."

"He can be a real troublemaker. Let me walk you to your car."

Tessa and Austin walked down the sidewalk in the opposite direction as Mac.

"Please don't tell Silas about this."

"Why?"

"I'm afraid of what he might do. He was furious the other night when that guy tried to talk to me at the restaurant."

"Yeah, when it comes to Silas and Mac, there's definitely no love between them. I won't say anything, but if he bothers you again, you need to say something to Silas."

"Maybe." They reached her car. "Thanks again, Austin. I'm glad you were around."

"You're welcome. Call me any time." Austin took a piece of paper out of his wallet and jotted down his phone number and handed it to her.

"Thanks."

* * *

WHEN Tessa heard Silas' truck pull into her driveway, she jumped off the couch and rushed to the door to greet him. He looked wonderful dressed in tight jeans and a brown flannel shirt. His hair, to her disappointment, his gorgeous long hair was pulled back into a ponytail. She wanted to run her fingers through that hair and pleasure him like she'd never done before. He stepped into the house.

"How was your trip?" she asked.

"It was tiring, and I'm glad to be home." He looked over and saw the flowers he'd sent. "The flowers still look nice."

"Yes, they've kept well this week."

"What happened to your hand?" He gently took her bandaged hand into his.

"Oh, it's nothing. I cut myself with a knife when I was doing dishes today. I went to the clinic and got a few stitches, but I'm fine."

He raised her hand to his lips and gently kissed each knuckle. "I need to apologize to you again. I'm so sorry about what you saw at the bar last week and about lying to you."

"Stop." She pulled her hand back. "Let's wait until after dinner before we start discussing anything."

"That's probably a good idea. Are you ready to go?"

"Let me get my jacket."

He held the kitchen door opened for her and lightly touched her back as they walked to his truck and helped her in.

Silas drove around curve after curve and turn after turn on a narrow road.

"You weren't kidding about your home being hard to find," she said.

"I told you I like my privacy."

He turned onto an even narrower road and around one more curve and then a rustic looking house appeared down the hill in front of them.

"We're here." When the truck neared the house, an outdoor light came on illuminating the whole front yard. She looked over at him. "I like my security too."

He turned off his truck and hurried around to help her out. Taking her hand, he led her to the porch where she heard a dog barking inside.

"I didn't know you had a dog."

"My first secret revealed. Austin took care of her this week and said he'd bring her home today before I got here." He smiled and unlocked the door. When it swung open, a medium size, white and blonde Brittany Spaniel rushed out and immediately sat in front of him, tail thumping the ground with her tongue hanging to one side.

"What's her name?"

"Keely. It means beautiful." Silas bent over and rubbed the dog's head. He waved his hand toward the yard and said, "Go." The dog sped off and was out of sight in seconds.

"Where's she going?"

"Out to her favorite tree." He pushed the door open. "Please come in."

Tessa entered first, followed by Silas who closed the door behind him. The inside of the cabin looked plain, but comfortable. It was definitely a man's home with a couch, recliner, table, and flat-screen TV.

"What about Keely?"

"What about her?"

"Are you going to leave her out there? Aren't there bears around?"

"She knows to stay away from them, and she'll let me know when she wants back in. Come on into the kitchen. I have dinner warming in a slow cooker."

"You have a slow cooker?"

"I do know how to cook more than grilled hamburgers."

"Apparently."

Silas led her to the kitchen at the rear of the house and something smelled wonderful. He held her chair at the table, which was already set with a candle in the middle waiting to be lit.

"What's on the menu tonight?"

"Beef Fried Rice." He lifted the lid of the crock and steam billowed out as he spooned the rice onto a platter and placed it on the table. "I'm going to have a beer. Would you like some wine or something non-alcoholic?"

"I think I'd like a beer also, if you don't mind."

He grabbed two glasses from the cabinet and two beers from the refrigerator and brought them to the table. He sat down and poured the beer for both of them. Lastly, he lit the candle. "Please help yourself to the rice."

Tessa filled her plate and Silas did the same. She took a bite. "Oh my gosh, this is really good. How did you learn to cook like this?"

"I spent a year in Japan when I was in the Army."

"How long were you in the Army?"

"Six years. What else do you want to know?" He took a long drink of his beer.

He wasn't kidding when he said he would answer all questions. Maybe he is ready to share about his life. "Where are you from?"

"Virginia."

"Do your parents still live there?"

"My parents passed away some time ago."

"I'm sorry. My parents passed away several years ago too. My inheritance is paying for my year here. What about siblings?"

"I have a younger brother still in Virginia."

"What's his name?"

"Kenny." He took a bite of his food.

"What does he do for a living?"

"He's in prison." Silas looked down.

"Oh." She felt foolish for asking.

"I don't want to talk about Kenny. You're supposed to ask about me, and I know there's one particular thing you want to ask me, so go ahead."

"You're right." She became very serious and nervous. She took a sip of her beer and then dabbed the corner of her mouth with the napkin. "Are you still poaching animals?"

He looked straight at her. His face showed no emotion. "Yes."

It hit her like a ton of bricks, and she didn't know why. She had suspected it for a while, and Austin had confirmed it earlier in the day. Somehow she held a little hope Silas would say no. "Why do you do that?"

He got up and went to the refrigerator to get himself another beer. This time, foregoing the glass and popping the cap, he drank it straight from the bottle. "It's all about money. I'm good at it, and I get paid well."

"By Martin Pratt?"

"Yes."

"I guess I still don't understand why you do it. You're such a talented carpenter. Can't you make a living with that?"

"Around here? Not really. Now, let me ask you something. Knowing the truth, does that change how you feel about me?"

She hadn't expected that and thought for a few seconds. "That's a tough question. I've grown to care for you deeply, but I don't approve of what you're doing at all. I'm so confused."

"Aren't you going to ask about what we're really here to discuss?"

She had been nervous about this all week. She wanted to know, but then again, she didn't. She took a deep breath and asked. "Okay, tell me about those women at the bar."

"I've gone over this in my mind a hundred times, and now I'm not sure how to begin."

"The truth is always a good start."

"You're right. Those two women were customers of Martin's. They're from out of state and wanted to hunt a big game animal. I took them into the mountains where they each shot an elk." He stopped to gulp down a drink of his beer. "I could tell I was in trouble when I met them. They were a little too friendly. That red-headed one couldn't keep her hands off of me during the whole drive to and from the hunt."

"From what I saw, she couldn't keep her hands off of you at the bar, either."

He grinned and looked down for a second. "When they got their animals, I took them back to the barn. They were really happy and wanted to celebrate, so they asked me to meet them at the bar. I swear I told them no, but Martin told me I had to go if I wanted keep my job."

"You still could have refused? You don't need this job."

"I do. I'm like everyone else who have bills to pay. I couldn't make my truck payment, let alone anything else without the money I make from Martin."

"Go on, finish your explanation about the girls."

"I hated having to break my date with you, but I had no choice. I knew I couldn't tell you the truth, so I lied and regretted it as soon as I did."

She didn't say a word, just looked at him.

"My plan was to meet with the ladies at the bar for only a short time, just long enough to keep Martin happy, and I wasn't going to sleep with them."

"Well, you almost got away with your little lie. If Mae hadn't called and suggested we go there for dinner that night, I would have never known about any of it."

"Mae asked you to go to that bar for dinner?"

"Yes, why?"

"No reason. It just doesn't seem like a place she'd want to go to."

"We weren't in the bar. We were in the family room, but I had a pretty good view of you sitting at the bar between those two women."

Silas took a hold of her hand. "Those women meant nothing to me. You are the only one in my life right now that means anything, and I really don't want to lose you." He brought her hand to his lips and kissed gently.

In her heart, she knew he was telling the truth. While she had watched him in the bar that night, she saw that the women were the ones making the advances, not Silas. However, she was pretty sure he enjoyed the attention those women gave him. What man wouldn't? But, she never saw him encouraging them.

"You have to understand how I felt that night when I saw you. You'd told me you were going to Knoxville, and then I see you with two women at a bar. How was I supposed to feel?"

"I completely understand, and I'm going to do my best to not fall into a situation like that again."

"If it happens again, you will tell me, won't you?"

"I promise. Just know that I don't want any other woman, but you."

She liked hearing him say those words and smiled a little.

He stood. "Let's go into the living room." He blew out the candle, took her by the hand, and led her to his couch where she sat, sinking down into the plush cushion. "It feels a little cool in here to me. How about you?"

"Yes, it's a little cool."

"I think I'll start a fire in the fireplace."

It didn't take long for him to get the fire going, and he placed the screen in front of the fireplace. A scratch at the door let them know that the dog wanted back in. Silas opened the door, and she walked in and over to Tessa. Keely sniffed her hand and then gave it a little lick before going to lie down on the dog bed near the fireplace.

Silas sat down next to Tessa and took her hand into his. "Would you be more accepting to our relationship if I told you I'll only be working for Martin for a short time longer?"

"Maybe. What happens then?"

"I'm hoping to have a new legitimate job soon."

A little hope sparked in her heart. "What kind of job?"

"I can't say. I don't want to jinx it."

"A lot can happen in a short time. You could get caught and go back to jail."

"I could be very careful and not get caught. I'm just asking for a little bit longer to get my life straightened out." He gave her hand a squeeze.

"I'll have some conditions."

"I thought you would," he chuckled.

"I want to know where you are, in case something should happen to you."

"Okay, I suppose I could do that."

"When I'm with you, no illegal stuff such as dead animals or skins, or anything like that in your truck."

"Agreed."

"And, when we're together, no guns."

"Tessa, I have to keep a gun with me."

"Not when you're with me. I'm not against guns, but you're a convicted felon, and I won't be around you if you have a gun."

"Fine, but just remember what would have happened if I hadn't had a gun on the day the bear attacked you."

"That won't happen again."

"Anything else?"

"One more. No more lying to me."

"You drive a hard bargain, but I'll do it all to keep you in my life."

He moved closer and wrapped his arms around her for a kiss. Slowly, they moved their way down on the couch until Tessa found Silas lying on top of her. His kisses were more intoxicating than the beer she had earlier. His tongue constantly probed her mouth with urgency. His free hand made its way under her sweater and slipped her bra up, freeing her breasts. He gently kneaded and stoked each breast causing her breathing to come in short gasps. With him on top of her, she could feel his growing erection. His kisses moved from her lips to her neck and to her earlobe.

"Tessa, will you spend the night with me?" he whispered into her ear.

His hot breath sent shivers up her spine. "Yes."

"We should probably move this to the bedroom then, don't you think?"

"I think that would be a great idea."

He took her by the hand, and they walked to his bedroom, closing the door behind them before Keely could follow.

They stood next to the bed in an embrace as he kissed her again. Only the moonlight lit the room. "I was gentle with you last time because of your injuries, but I can't promise it will be the same this time."

"I need to feel you inside of me so bad," she said.

"We need to get rid of your clothes first." He grabbed the bottom of her sweater and peeled it off over her head, tossing it somewhere in the room. "You're not going to need this." He reached behind her to rid her of her bra. "Now, the most important part." He unbuttoned her jeans and let them drop to the floor. She kicked off her shoes and stepped out of the pants and panties.

"You're so beautiful, and I want you so badly," he said, capturing her lips again.

She broke the kiss off. "My turn."

She slowly opened each button on his shirt, keeping constant eye contact with him until all the buttons were unfastened, and he shed his shirt. He started to remove his pants, but she stopped him. "Not so fast. I'm not finished with you above your waist yet."

First, she reached behind his head and pulled his hair loose. "I love your long hair." She ran her fingers through it as she kissed him again. Then, starting at his shoulders, she slowly ran her hands down and over his broad smooth chest, barely touching him. He shuttered as her fingertips skimmed over his skin. "Now your pants." First unbuckling his belt, she then unbuttoned his pants, and while kissing his stomach, unzipped the fly. With a quick tug down, his pants dropped releasing his engorged member. "Oh my, commando style," she said.

She gently took his shaft into her hand and began massaging. He let out a groan looking skyward. Lowering herself to her knees, she took him into her mouth. He grabbed her head to help keep his balance, while at the same time keeping her at the perfect angle. "Oh God!" he murmured, continuing his stare at the ceiling.

She could tell he was about to come. She stood up, and he wasted no time in laying her on the bed and crawling on top of her. His skin was warm against her. His hands were all over her body, and he covered her with kisses from her lips to her breast. His hand finally made its way to the dampness between her legs. She let out a gasp as he entered not one, but two fingers. His movements were quick and hard, bringing her to the edge quickly. "Silas, now. Please, I need you now."

He replaced his hard fingers with his even harder arousal and entered her with a driving thrust. She moaned in pleasure. He sank himself into her again and again until he exploded inside of her, and she let out an uninhibited cry of ecstasy. They both gasped for air until their breathing found its own rhythm and slowed. Tessa felt the cool air against her damp skin and shivered.

"You're cold."

"Just a little."

He pulled out of her and pulled the sheet and blankets up over them. Lying back down, he put his arm around her, and she laid her head against his chest. She could hear his heart pounding from the exertion while he rubbed her arm.

"Silas?"

"Yeah."

"I've fallen in love with you."

He held her even tighter and kissed the top of her head. "I love you too."

She kissed his chest. After making love for a second time, they both fell asleep in each other's arms.

Sometime in the middle of the night, Tessa heard Silas' cell phone ring a few times before he woke up and answered it.

"Hello," he mumbled. "Now? What time is it?"

She looked at the clock by the bed that showed two in the morning.

"Okay, I'll be there in about thirty minutes." He tossed his phone back on the table.

"What's going on?" she asked.

"I have to go out for a little while."

"Where?"

"You don't want to know." He got out of bed and walked around the room picking up his clothes that had been quickly tossed aside earlier. Tessa enjoyed the view of his naked body moving about the room. "You promised that you'd tell me whenever you go somewhere," she reminded him.

He pulled his jeans on and zipped them closed. "You're right. Someone broke into Martin's barn where he conducts his business. They want me to come in and help figure out what's missing."

He buttoned his shirt and pulled a knit hat on his head. Leaning down, he gave her a kiss. "Keep the bed warm and I'll be back as fast as I can." He opened the door and nearly tripped over Keely sleeping on the floor. The dog jumped up. "Keely, stay with Tessa." The dog walked into the bedroom and jumped up on the bed, curling up at her feet. "I hope you don't mind."

"I don't mind. I kind of like her in here with me while you're gone."

"I won't be long."

He grabbed his keys and left through the front door.

* * * * *

CHAPTER 6

SILAS started his truck and drove away from his house. It was a cold night, and he hoped the truck cab would warm soon. He hated leaving Tessa alone in his bed. Lying next to her tonight felt so right, and he was happy they could admit their love for each other. He'd never told a woman he loved her before. It was something new to him and felt good. He only hoped their relationship would hold strong during the next few months.

"Damn." He felt around his pockets and realized he had left his cell phone on the table next to the bed, and he didn't want Tessa snooping through the files or numbers he had in it. He had been driving for about twenty minutes and made a u-turn in the middle of the road. Heading back to his house, an uneasy feeling crept over him. He couldn't explain it, but something wasn't right.

As he got closer to the house, his fear was validated. An orange glow lit the sky above the tree line. As he turned the last curve, he saw it. His house was on fire. "Tessa."

He pushed the accelerator to the floor and slid to a stop when he reached the house. Flames were already coming through the roof and covered the front door. He could see through the window that the fire had spread throughout the living room. "Tessa!"

He heard something from inside the house. Keely was barking from the bedroom. Silas went to the side of the house to the bedroom window, but couldn't see anything but smoke inside. "Tessa!" Keely's barking was getting weaker. He had to get in there.

Taking off his jacket and wrapping it around his arm, he hit the window several times until the glass shattered. Smoke poured out as he broke more of the glass to get inside. "Tessa! Tessa, where are you?"

Quickly climbing through the broken window, he cut his hand on the edge of the jagged glass. He pulled off his knit hat and used it to cover his nose and mouth. The smoke stung his eyes as he went low in the room making his way to the bed to find Tessa, but she wasn't there. The knit hat did little to keep the smoke from his lungs, and through his coughs, he still called out for her.

Keely was no longer barking, but he could hear the dog whimpering on the other side of the bed. Silas crawled around the bed and found both

Tessa and the dog on the floor next to the bedroom door. He could feel the heat from the door and knew the fire would break through any minute. "Tessa, can you hear me?" She was unconscious. He pulled the blanket off of the bed and wrapped it around her and picked her up, making his way back to the window. "Come on, Keely. Follow me, girl."

Careful not to hurt her on the glass, Silas cautiously climbed out the window and carried Tessa as far from the house as he could and laid her on the ground. He could still feel the heat from the burning structure. Tessa was breathing, but barely. Silas rushed back to the house to get his dog and found her on the floor by the window. He pulled Keely through just as the bedroom door imploded with a burst of fire. He carried the dog over next to Tessa as the fire trucks pulled up to the house. Silas also collapsed next to Tessa gasping for his own breath.

The firemen jumped out of the trucks and started pulling hoses from the truck and attaching them before pouring water on the fully engulfed house. There would be no saving the structure. An ambulance followed the fire trucks and stopped near them. Two emergency medical technicians came running over. "What happened?"

"She's unconscious and barely breathing. I found her on the floor of the bedroom," Silas said between his own coughs.

A fireman brought the stretcher over along with a bottle of oxygen and placed the mask on Tessa's face. Then he came over to check on Silas.

"Get away from me! Take care of her first."

"How long has she been unconscious, sir?" one of the EMTs asked.

"I don't know. I had been gone for about forty minutes and when I got back, I found the house burning. I broke the window to get her and my dog out."

Both EMT's continued to check her over. "What's her name?" one of them asked.

"Tessa."

"Tessa, Tessa honey, can you hear me? Come on, Tessa. You need to wake up," the EMT said. There was no response.

"Her blood pressure is low and breathing is shallow with a weak pulse. We need to get her to the hospital right away."

The fireman and one of the EMT's prepared her for loading onto the stretcher.

The other EMT walked over to Silas. "Sir, let me take a look at your hand."

"What?"

"Your hand, sir. It looks like you've cut it."

Silas looked at his bloody hand and held it out for the EMT, but kept his eye on Tessa. "Is she going to be all right?"

"It looks like she's taken in a lot of smoke. They won't know how bad until they get her to the hospital."

A firefighter came over to them. "What happened here tonight?"

Silas was still coughing, but said, "I got called away around two o'clock, but forgot something. I turned around, and when I got back, the house was already burning."

"What's your name?"

He hesitated for a split second. "Silas Newberry."

"We need to get them both to the hospital," the EMT told the fireman.

They lifted Tessa onto the stretcher and quickly loaded her into the ambulance. Silas and the other EMT followed.

"I'll finish bandaging your hand in the ambulance. Get in," the EMT told Silas.

Before getting into the ambulance, he looked back at his dog and saw a fireman giving her oxygen too. "Don't worry about your dog. I'll take care of her," the fireman said.

He gave the firefighter a nod and climbed into the back of the vehicle and sat next to Tessa. She looked so pale and lifeless. The door closed and the ambulance moved, siren blaring.

"How did you cut your hand, sir?" the EMT said while applying the bandage.

"I cut it when I climbed through the broken window to get her out. She's still unconscious. Shouldn't she be awake by now?"

"She inhaled a lot of smoke. They'll need to run some tests on her at the hospital to make sure her lungs aren't damaged. There's not much we can do here, but keep the oxygen on her. That's the main thing she needs right now."

Silas started coughing again.

"How much smoke did you breath in?"

"I don't know."

"Here, you should put this mask on too." He handed Silas an oxygen mask.

"No, I'll be fine."

"Sir, you may think you're fine, but smoke inhalation can be a silent killer. Please take the oxygen."

Silas took the mask and started breathing in the clean air.

When they arrived at the hospital, things moved very fast. The doors to the ambulance opened to nurses and emergency workers who immediately took Tessa inside. Silas tried to follow, but they ushered him into another room so he could be examined. "Wait, I need to go with her."

"We'll keep you updated on her condition, but you need to be checked out too," the nurse said. "Let me take a look at that hand."

The nurse cleaned his wound, which was beginning to hurt. After what seemed like a long wait, the doctor finally came in to stitch Silas' hand.

"How is my girlfriend?" Silas asked.

The doctor looked at the nurse. "She's the smoke inhalation patient."

"Oh." The doctor looked back at Silas. "I'm not the doctor treating her, but I believe they are waiting for the results of her chest x-ray and blood gases before starting treatment. You'll be informed as soon as her doctor knows something."

The doctor finished the stitches and left, and the nurse applied a fresh bandage. Silas was taken down for a chest x-ray then. Upon returning, his oxygen level was checked again, and he was given some painkillers for his hand. They released him from care around seven o'clock in the morning.

"What about Tessa? How is she?" he asked the nurse.

"She regained consciousness and has been taken to a room. She's going to be fine, but it will be a few days before she'll start feeling like herself again. She's going to need a lot of rest."

"What room is she in?" He needed to see her. He needed to see she really was okay. He felt responsible because he wasn't there for her when the fire started.

The nurse checked the computer and directed him to the appropriate elevator. He rushed down the hallway and on the way ran into Austin.

"Silas, what happened? I got a call that your house burned, and you and Tessa were brought in here."

"I'm not sure what happened. Mac called me around two this morning and said someone broke into the barn, and Martin wanted me to come in to help see what was missing. I forgot my phone, and when I got back to get it, the house was on fire. I was only gone about forty minutes. What if it was my fault? What if I didn't cover the fireplace well enough and a spark caused the fire?"

"I'm sure it's not your fault. You're always careful about that. Is Tessa okay?"

"She was in my bed when I left. When I got back and saw the fire, I had to break the window to get inside and found her unconscious on the floor. They told me she's going to be okay, but I won't believe it until I see her."

"Wait, you said someone broke into the barn?"

"Yeah."

"No one called me about that, and I was there until about midnight last night."

"That fucking Mac. Would you come back and pick me up here in about an hour? I'm going to go check on Tessa and then go back to what's left of my house. Something's going on."

"I'll be here," Austin said.

Silas took the elevator to the second floor and found Tessa's room. He stepped in and saw that she was sleeping. She still looked so pale with an IV attached to her arm and an oxygen tube under her nose. He quietly went in, pulled the chair next to her bed, and sat down. He took her hand into his and watched her as she slept. She stirred and opened her eyes. "Silas? What happened? Where am I?" she whispered, her voice raspy from the smoke.

"You don't remember?"

"The doctor told me there was a fire, but I don't remember."

Her voice sounded so weak. "Do you remember me leaving the house in the middle of the night?"

"Yes, after the phone call."

"Right. I left the house, but I forgot my phone. When I came back to get it, the house was on fire, and you were still inside."

"I remember now. Keely started barking after you left, and I woke up with the room full of smoke. I could barely breathe. I went to the bedroom door, but it was too hot to open. That's the last thing I remember. How did I get out?" She started coughing.

Silas waited until she stopped. "I broke the window in the bedroom and found you on the floor and carried you out."

"Keely, is she okay?"

"I don't know, but I got her out too. When I got in the ambulance with you, a fireman was giving her oxygen."

Tessa looked at his bandage. "What happened to your hand?"

"Oh, it's nothing. I cut it on the window."

"You realize you saved my life again?"

"I shouldn't have left in the first place. If I'd stayed instead of running off like I did, you wouldn't be in here. I'm so sorry, Tessa."

"It's not your fault, and if you hadn't left and came back when you did, we both might have burned up. Do they know how it started?"

"No, but I'm going back out there today and look around. Austin's picking me up and I'll talk to the fire chief to see if his department came up with anything."

Her eyes looked droopy, and she nearly fell asleep as he spoke.

"Find out about Keely too," she said, drifting back off to sleep.

"I will, and I'll be back later. I love you, Tessa." He kissed her on the check and left.

When Silas stepped out of the room, he ran into a woman wearing scrubs and looked at the ID she wore. "Are you Tessa's doctor?"

"Yes, I'm Dr. Johnson, and you are?"

"Silas Newberry."

"Ah, yes, Mr. Newberry. She kept asking for you last night."

"How is she?"

"Technically, you're not related to her, so…."

"I'm the closest thing to family she has right now."

The doctor thought for a few seconds and then began. "She inhaled a lot of smoke last night. Her oxygen level dropped below eighty-eight percent. That's very dangerous. We've brought it up to—" She looked at the chart she held. "Ninety-three percent. That's not the best, but it's much better."

"Was there any permanent damage?"

"There's been no indication of that, but we're going to keep her on oxygen until tomorrow. Once her level has reached ninety-five percent, she can go home."

"Thank you. That's good to hear. I'll be back later to see her."

Austin was waiting out in front of the hospital when Silas came out of the door. They drove out to what was left of his house. A fire truck, a couple cars, and a police car were parked in the yard. A few firemen were still spraying water on some hot spots where wisps of smoke rose from the rubble. Austin shut off his truck and they walked over to join the group of men.

They stood looking at what was left of his home, which wasn't much more than the concrete slab it had sat on. The smell of burnt wood and smoke filled the air.

One of the firemen and two other gentlemen walked up to them. "Mr. Newberry?"

"Yes."

"I'm Chief Barnes with the fire department. This is Deputy Whitman and Doyle Greene with the State Fire Marshal's office."

"Hello, gentleman." He shook hands with them.

"We were looking though what's left of your cabin," Chief Banes said.

"Were you home when the fire started?" Greene asked.

"No, I had gotten call from a friend who needed some help and was on my way to help him. When I realized I forgot my cell phone, I turned around to go back to get it. The fire was burning when I returned."

"You were the one that got Miss Cooper out?" the chief asked.

"Yes. Why?"

"This fire was intentionally set," Greene said.

"What!"

"Come with me and I'll show you." They walked over to where his front door had been. "The source of the fire was here." He pointed to the floor. It appears that someone squirted lighter fluid under the door and then lit it."

"How do you know that?" Austin asked.

"Joe, bring that hose over here," the chief called. The other fireman brought the hose to the chief who started spraying water on the concrete slab that had been the floor. When he shut the hose off, the water showed an oily looking pattern as if something had been poured on the floor from the door.

"I took a reading with our sniffer machine it detected an accelerant. The result was lighter fluid," Greene said.

"Someone tried to kill us?" Silas asked.

"We don't think so," the fire chief said.

The State Fire Marshal explained further. "You said you were back within about forty minutes?"

"That's right."

"For the fire to progress as quickly as you described, it had to have been set as soon as you left the house. Assuming it wasn't you that started the fire, someone may have been here waiting for you to leave."

"You think I started the fire? Tessa was in there. I would never do anything to hurt her."

"Mr. Newberry, you said a friend called you for some help last night," the deputy said, taking out a small notebook. "Who was that friend?"

"Mac Conrad."

"Do you have his number for me to call and confirm that?"

"I'm sorry, but my phone burned up in the house, and I don't remember his number," Silas said. He looked at Austin.

"I don't know his number, either."

"Does he live around here?" the deputy asked.

"Yes, in a little shack up on White Cloud Hill."

"Do you know anyone who would want to do this to you, or anyone you've had any problems with lately?"

Silas looked at Austin and then back to the deputy. "I work as a carpenter, I'm sure there have been some customers that haven't been satisfied with my work, but no one has threatened me."

"If you think of anything, please give me a call at the Sheriff's Department and don't forget that I'll need Mr. Conrad's phone number as soon as possible," the deputy said.

"Of course. Thank you," Silas replied.

"Oh, Mr. Newberry, about your dog," the chief said.

"What about her? Is she okay?"

"Yes, she's fine. One of my men took her back to the firehouse, and Doc Jones checked her out. We have her there, if you wouldn't mind coming to pick her up."

"I'll stop by later today. Thank you."

The three investigators got into their cars and left. The other firemen had finished their watering of the burned building and were loading the hoses back onto the truck.

Silas turned to Austin. "I have a problem."

"What's going on?"

"I think I know who set the fire."

"Who?"

"Mac. We had a little altercation."

"What? That little scuffle you two had at the barn?"

"That was just the beginning. Tessa and I ran into him at Joe's Barbecue one night. He was drunk, and I had to put him down in the parking lot when he tried to get close to Tessa. After I took her home, I went over to his house, punched him out, and told him I'd kill him if he ever came near her again."

"Well, it's a good bet he lured you out of the house so he could set it on fire," Austin said. "He probably didn't even know Tessa was inside."

"I'm going to kill that son of a bitch." He turned and started toward his truck.

"Wait." Austin grabbed Silas by the arm. "You don't want to make this worse than it already is."

"It's already worse. Mac is never going to tell the police he called me last night, and he probably used a burner phone so they can't trace it. I'll have no alibi, and it'll look like I did it. I'm going to have to take care of this myself."

"At least let me go with you."

"Fine. They're probably at the barn by now. I'm anxious to find out if someone really did break in there last night."

The two men got into their trucks and drove over to Martin's barn.

They walked inside and found Mac, Greg, and a few other men sitting at the table drinking beer.

"Hey, look who's here. Sit down and have a beer, Silas," Mac said. "I heard you had a little problem out at your place last night."

"You ought to know," Silas said, his hands curled into fists while trying to keep his temper under control.

Mac sniffed the air with his nose. "You smell like smoke, buddy. You should go home and take a shower. Oh wait, you don't have a home to go to now, do you?" He laughed.

That was all it took. Silas pulled Mac out of the chair by his collar. "You son of a bitch, you burned my house down last night, didn't you?"

"Let go of me. I didn't do anything."

"Both of you settle down?" Martin shouted coming out of his office.

Silas threw Mac back down into his chair. "Someone set my house on fire last night and burned it to the ground right after Mac called me to come in here because the barn had been broken in."

"Someone did break in here last night," Martin said. The other men in the room mumbled their agreement.

"I'm sorry to hear about your house, son. Is there anything I can do?"

"My house can be replaced, but Tessa was inside."

"What? Is she okay?" Martin asked.

"Yeah, I forgot my phone and got back in time to get her out, but she's in the hospital right now with smoke inhalation."

"Silas, man, I'm sorry to hear about your girlfriend, but I had nothing to do with it," Mac said.

"The hell you didn't." He started toward Mac again.

Martin stepped between them. "Now, calm down."

"The police asked where I was, and I told them you called me out to help you with something," he said to Mac over Martin's shoulder. "I'm their first suspect, so you damn well better confirm my story!" He pointed his finger at Mac.

"He'll confirm your story. I'll see to it," Martin said. "You need to calm down and get some rest. I bet you've been awake since the fire and worried about Tessa on top of that."

"I'm fine." He still glared at Mac.

"Austin, can you take him somewhere to get a shower and some sleep?"

"Yes, sir. He can come to my place."

"I'll make sure Mac does the right thing." Martin reached into his pocket and pulled out a wad of money. He peeled off three one hundred dollar bills and put them into Silas' hand. "Go buy whatever you need and get some rest."

"I appreciate it, but I really don't need it." He tried to give the money back.

"Son, you just lost practically everything you own in a fire. Take the money and get you some clothes."

"Thanks." He shook Martin's hand.

"Come on, buddy," Austin said, taking Silas by the arm. "Let's get you to a shower."

The two men walked outside.

"I know he did it," Silas said.

"You're probably right, but we can't prove it, at least not yet. Come on over to my place. Martin was right about one thing, you need to take a shower and get some sleep."

"I need to stop by the firehouse and get Keely first."

Silas got into his truck and drove away from the barn and straight to the firehouse. Several of the firemen were standing outside when he drove up and parked. As soon as he stepped out of his truck, he heard barking. He looked up, and Keely was running toward him.

"Hey, girl. How are you?" The dog jumped up on him, happy to see him. He walked over to the firemen.

"I want to thank you guys for taking care of my dog. When I left in the ambulance with Tessa last night, I wasn't sure if I was going to see Keely again."

"She's a good dog and was no problem at all," one of the firemen said. "Doc Jones stopped by to check on her. He said she inhaled a lot of smoke, but the oxygen she got on the scene helped. I think she's made a full recovery already."

"How much do I owe Doc Jones?"

"It's been taken care of," another fireman said.

"I can't let you guys do that."

"It's what we do. How's the lady that was in your house?"

"She's still in the hospital resting. They don't expect any permanent damage."

"She's a lucky lady."

"Yes, she is." Silas wondered if they were insinuating he had started the fire, and she was lucky to get out.

"I better get Keely out of your hair. Thanks again."

Silas and Keely got into his truck and left. He really did need to stop and buy some new clothes and a new phone, but everything was beginning to catch up to him. It was all he could do to keep his eyes open. He had a change of clothes in his truck, and that would have to do until after he got some sleep.

Austin lived in town, and Silas was at his apartment within a few minutes. Both he and Keely went inside. Silas put his bag of clothes on the floor, and the dog ran to Austin.

"Hi, Keely. You're lookin' good, girl," Austin said, petting the dog and then looked at Silas. "You, on the other hand, look like hell."

"It's really hitting me now."

"I made some sandwiches, if you're hungry."

"I am, but I'm too tired to eat. I really just want a shower and to crash on your couch for a few hours."

"There are towels in the bathroom and a blanket and pillow already on the couch for you. I've got to go into the store for a few hours. I'll leave the sandwiches in the refrigerator. If you want, I'll take Keely with me so you can sleep."

"They don't mind having a dog in the store?"

"Nope. Dogs are in there all the time."

"That would be great. Thanks."

"Come on, Keely. You're going to love being at the store," Austin said.

He and the dog went out the door, and Silas headed for the shower. Even the warm water flowing over his body couldn't revive him. He was dog tired when he got out, and dried himself off. He forgot all about the sandwich in the refrigerator, and went straight to couch falling asleep instantly.

After sleeping for several hours, Silas drove back to the hospital to see Tessa. He knocked on the door to her hospital room.

"Come in."

He stepped in and found her eating dinner and felt relived to see she looked much better than she did when he had left her that morning, but she still had the oxygen tube under her nose. He walked over and gave her a kiss. "How are you feeling?"

"Much better. How about you? How's your hand?"

"It's fine. The stitches are already starting to itch, so I guess it's healing." He sat down next to her bed.

"Did you find anything out about the how the fire started?"

He decided it was too soon to tell her about him being an arson suspect. "Nothing yet."

"The doctor thinks I can go home tomorrow."

"That's good to hear." He took her hand and kissed it. "I'm so sorry you were in the fire."

"It's not your fault. Accidents happen. I'm just glad you forgot your phone and came back to save me."

"I'm not sure what I would have done if something would have happened to you." He fought back a tear. He was emotional at the thought of losing her and didn't want her to see him cry. What guy cries? That's when it hit him just how important she was, and it scared him. "I probably should let you rest. I'll be back in the morning.

"You're leaving already?"

"You need to rest so you can go home tomorrow." He cupped her chin with his hand and kissed her again before leaving.

* * * * *

CHAPTER 7

TESSA sat up in bed watching some television, having just finished her respiratory therapy exercises.

The oxygen tube still hung under her nose, but she felt so much better and was anxious to get home. She was even more anxious to see Silas. She heard a knock at her door and hoped he had come to take her home. The door opened, but instead of Silas, it was Dr. Johnson. Tessa picked up the remote control and turned off the television.

"Good morning, Tessa."

"Good morning."

"How are you feeling?"

"Much better. I'm hoping I can go home today."

Dr. Johnson looked through the file she held. "I'm pleased to see that your oxygen level has increased greatly, and I also see that you did well in your therapy this morning." She took her stethoscope and listened to Tessa's lungs. "Deep breath." She moved to the other lung. "Again." She then took her finger and lifted each eyelid to look at her eyes. "I think we can discard your oxygen now." The doctor carefully removed the oxygen tube that Tessa wore around her head and turned it off.

"That feels so much better," Tessa said.

"How does your chest feel?"

"Still a little irritated."

"How is your coughing?"

"Not as bad as it was yesterday."

"That's good. There's not really any kind of medication we give to smoke inhalation victims, but there are two things you can do at home, keep up with your therapy exercises and use a saline nasal spray to keep your sinus membranes moist. You can find bottles of that at any pharmacy. You don't need a prescription, and you can't overdose with it. You should use it often."

"Does that mean I can go home?"

"It does. You can leave anytime. Do you have someone that can come to get you?"

"Silas can take me, but since it was his house that burned, he probably has more pressing things to take care of."

"I'm sure he'll be here soon. I spoke with him yesterday morning, and he seemed very concerned about you."

"He's very special to me. I supposed I could call my neighbor, Mae, to come get me if Silas doesn't get here soon."

"Don't wait too long, you need to get home and start recovering. I'll tell the nurse to start getting your discharge paperwork ready. You should follow up with your regular doctor in a few days."

"I don't have a regular doctor. I just moved down here a few months ago. The only time I needed to see a doctor, I went to the clinic in town."

"I supposed you could follow up with them. Just make sure they check your records through the hospital record system. Good luck, Tessa."

"Thank you, Dr. Johnson."

Anxious to get out of the hospital, Tessa wished she could call Silas, but had no idea how to get a hold of him since his phone burned in the fire. For that matter, her phone burned too, and she didn't even know Mae's number. She'd have to ask the nurse to find it for her. Then, she noticed the door slowly open, and Silas' head appeared around it.

"Can I come in?"

"Yes, come in. I've been hoping you'd come soon."

"I didn't want to wake you, in case you were sleeping." He walked over and gave her a hug and a kiss. He carried a plastic grocery sack and sat it on the floor. "You look even better today."

"The doctor just left and said I can go home. I was sitting here trying to figure out how I was going to do that. Can you take me?"

"I'd be happy to take you home." He pulled the chair next to the bed and sat down.

She rang for the nurse and then told her over the intercom that she was ready to leave. She looked back at Silas. "How bad is your cabin?"

"It's gone, burned completely down."

"Oh no, I'm so sorry. Do you know what happened?"

"The fire department has some theories, but we can talk about that later."

"What about Keely?"

"She's fine. The firemen had the local vet check her out. Austin has her at his apartment."

The nurse knocked on the door and came in carrying several sheets of paper. Silas moved the chair back while the nurse went over all of Tessa's discharge instructions. "Once you're dressed, I'll bring in the wheelchair, and we can get you out of here," the nurse said.

"Dressed? I—well, I wasn't wearing any clothes when I was brought in." Tessa felt her face flush. "It was the middle of the night, and I was sleeping when the fire started."

"We can probably find you some scrubs to wear."

"Actually, I brought her something to wear," Silas said, picking up the plastic sack.

"You did?"

"I knew you didn't have anything, so I stopped by your house and got some clothes for you."

"How did you get inside?" Silas cocked his head to one side and raised his eyebrows. "Oh!" She remembered his breaking and entering conviction.

The nurse left, and Silas handed the bag of clothes to Tessa. "I hope I brought the right things."

Tessa got out of bed and took the bag into the bathroom to change. A few minutes later, she stepped out smiling. "I see that you brought my sexiest lingerie."

"Well, I didn't know what you liked, but I knew what I liked." He took her into his arms and kissed her, but she immediately started coughing. He jumped back. "I'm sorry. I shouldn't have done that."

"No, it's okay." She coughed hard, but then it passed. "I'm fine now."

The nurse came in pushing a wheelchair, and Silas left to meet them at the front door with his truck. Tessa sat in the wheelchair and rode to the front door of the hospital where they found Silas waiting. He got out and helped her into the truck.

As soon as they were out of the parking lot and on the road, Silas spoke up. "I'm sorry about what happened with the fire. It was my fault."

"What do you mean it was your fault? Did you do something that started the fire?"

"Not directly. The fire chief said someone was probably waiting for me to leave and then started it. I'm pretty sure it was Mac, but I don't think he knew you were in there."

"Mac? The guy you punched out in the parking lot?"

"That's him. I didn't want you to know, but after I dropped you off at your house that night, I went to see him. I told him that if he came near you again, I'd kill him."

"Silas, you didn't?"

"My problem with Mac started way before that night. We haven't liked each other from the very start, but I had no idea he would do something this bad."

"Will he try anything else?"

"I don't think so, but there's another problem."

"What's that?"

"I'm the prime suspect for starting the fire."

"You didn't do it."

"I know, but Mac is my alibi. He's the one that called me out. All he has to do is say he didn't, and I'm sunk."

"What about phone records?"

"He probably used a burner phone that can't be traced back to him. The police will say I called my own phone to set up my alibi. Tessa, they'll want to talk to you about it."

"I'll tell them you didn't do it."

"Thanks, but it's going to take more than your statement, I'm afraid."

"Can we drive over to your house? I'd like to see it or what's left of it?"

They were near the road to his home, so he turned and headed up the road. When they rounded the last turn, Tessa saw the burnt ruins. "Oh my, we were in that."

He pulled the truck to a stop in the yard and got out. He helped Tessa out of the truck and held her hand as they walked toward the rubble.

"Yeah, I'm going to have to find a new place to live."

"You can move in with me."

He stopped and turned to look at her. "I can't do that."

"Why not?"

"Well, I—" He was silent for a few seconds. "I just can't."

"That's not a very good reason. Where did you stay last night?"

"I slept on Austin's couch."

"If I remember correctly, he said at my cookout on Labor Day that he lived in a small apartment, and I have a cabin with lots of room for both you and Keely."

After a clap of thunder, a drizzle of rain started coming down. "Let's get back into the truck and get you home. I don't want you to get sick," he said.

Once in the truck, he started the engine and headed toward Tessa's. The quiet ride to her house gave her time to think about Silas moving in with her. If he moved in, maybe she could persuade him to stop working for Martin.

The rain was coming down harder when they reached her house. "I don't suppose you have an umbrella in here, do you?" she asked.

Silas chuckled. "It's not something I use regularly."

"I guess we'll have to make a run for it then." She started to open the truck door, but he reached over her and closed it.

"What are you doing?" he asked.

"I'm trying to go to my house."

"Are you crazy? You'll get soaked. Do you want to get pneumonia?"

"I'm not going to get sick."

"You're lungs are still irritated from the smoke. You need to take it easy."

"Maybe I need someone to stay here and watch over me then." She opened the truck door and jumped out, running to the kitchen door under an overhanging roof.

She immediately started coughing as soon as she stopped. Silas followed and put his arm around her and held her until her coughing finally ceased.

"Can you open the door?" she asked, slightly out of breath.

"It's locked," he said.

"I know. My key burned up with my purse in your house. You got in there once. Can't you do it again?"

He just shook his head. "Wait here." He ran back to his truck and fumbled to get something out of the back seat. He came back with a small pouch in his hand. He used two small tools that looked like files and in a matter of seconds he had the door unlocked.

"How did you do that?" she asked, stepping inside.

"You don't want to know. Do you have another key inside, or do we need to call your landlord?"

"I have another one in the bedroom." She sat down at the kitchen table to catch her breath.

"Are you okay?"

"I'm fine, just a little out of breath."

"Come on, let's get you to bed."

"You just can't wait, can you?" she joked.

"You know what I mean. You need your rest."

"I'd rather curl up on the couch, wrapped in a blanket with some hot tea and my favorite guy."

He smiled. "I think I can arrange that." He walked with her into the living room and sat her on the couch where a blanket was draped over the back to cover her. "Where's your tea?"

"There's a box in the cabinet next to the refrigerator." She could hear him rummaging around in the kitchen and wondered how much trouble fixing a cup of tea could be. "Do you need some help?"

"No, I got it," he called from the kitchen.

She didn't have to wait long before he walked back in carrying a tray with two cups of hot tea and a plate of cookies. He sat the tray on the coffee table in front of the couch.

"You did good." She took a bite of a cookie. "Sit next to me."

He sat down, and she moved the blanket over both of them. She brushed back his long hair and kissed him on the cheek.

"Maybe there's a movie on TV we can watch," he suggested and grabbed the remote control.

"Wait. We need to decide something first. Are you going to move in here or not?"

"I thought that was settled. It's not a good idea."

"Tell me why." She sipped her drink.

"I couldn't live with myself if something happened to you again because of me. If there's a chance my being here might put you in jeopardy, then I won't do it."

"What if he decides to do something to me anyway and you're not here to protect me?"

He didn't say anything.

"You know I'm right."

"I know, but—"

She interrupted. "I'm not taking no for an answer."

"If I did stay here, it would only be until I found a place of my own to move to."

"Good, it's settled then. Now, I have some things I need to do tomorrow. Do you think you could take me?"

"Oh, I see now. You want me to move in so I can wait on you," he teased.

"I need to get a new cell phone, and you probably need one too. I also need to figure out how I can get a copy of my driver's license since it burned up too."

"I'll take you anywhere you need to go tomorrow. Today, you need to settle in on the couch in my arms and get some rest." He took her cup and set it on the tray, put his arm around her and drew her closer to him. He pushed the button on the remote control and started surfing the channels for a movie to watch. They spent the rest of the day watching old movies.

* * *

TESSA woke up the next morning and reached for Silas on the other side of the bed, but he wasn't there. He must have already got up. "Silas?" No answer.

She got out of bed, slipped on her robe, and walked down the hallway to the kitchen. She looked in the living room on the way. No Silas. In the kitchen, she found a note on the table from him. It said he was gone to Austin's to get Keely and would be back soon.

There was hot coffee in the coffeemaker, so she poured herself a cup and went to the living room, and sat at her computer. She needed to email Sara and let her know what had happened. Before she had a chance to open her email program, she heard a knock at the door that startled her. What if it was Mac looking for Silas?

Before going to the door, she looked out the window, but didn't see a car in the driveway. She went to the door. "Who is it?"

"It's Mae, dear. I just wanted to check to see if you were okay."

Relieved, Tessa opened the door. "Hi, Mae. Please come in." The older lady stepped inside. Tessa closed the door behind her and locked it. "Would you like some coffee?"

"That would be nice, but sit down, honey. I can get it."

Rather than argue with Mae, knowing she wouldn't win, Tessa sat down.

"I heard what happened to you. Are you feeling better?" Mae asked, pouring her coffee.

"Yes, I'm much better. I still have a little cough, but that will eventually disappear. How did you hear about it?"

"Elaine Pratt told me and there was that article in the newspaper." She sat down at the table with Tessa.

"What article?"

"There's an article in today's paper about the fire and how you were inside and pulled out by Silas. It also says Silas is suspected of starting the fire himself so he could rescue you."

"That's ridiculous. Silas did not start the fire."

"I thought you were finished with him after you caught him with those women at the bar."

"It's a long story, but he and I had a long talk, and he explained everything."

"He did, did he? So he told you that he's mixed up with Martin Pratt?"

"Yes, and that in a few months, he'll have a new legitimate job. No more criminal stuff."

"What kind of job did he say he was going to have?" She took a drink of her coffee.

"He didn't say. He wanted to wait until he knew for sure about it before telling me."

"You believed him?"

"I do believe him. He's a good man and, in fact, he's moving in here with me."

"What?"

"At least until he finds another place to live, but I'm hoping he'll stay permanently." Tessa hated that Mae was constantly putting Silas down and knew she was only concerned about her well being, but she wasn't going to talk her out of a relationship with him.

"I'm going into town later. Do you need anything, dear?"

Tessa was grateful Mae dropped the subject of her and Silas. "No, Silas is taking me later, but thanks for the offer."

"I had better get going and let you get some rest. Now, you let me know if you need anything."

"I will. Thanks." She walked Mae to the door, closing and locking it after her.

Back in the living room, she finally opened her email program and saw several messages from Sara. She read them and responded with one long email explaining everything that happened and that she would call her as soon as she got a new phone.

Tessa lay down on the couch to watch some television, but drifted off to sleep. She awoke when she heard someone coming in the kitchen door. "Silas, is that you?"

When he walked into the living room, she noticed he stuffed something into his back pocket. "It's me. Sorry if I woke you."

"That's okay." She got up and gave him a hug and in doing so she grabbed what he had put in his pocket.

Silas quickly spun around and grabbed her wrist in a tight grip.

"Ouch! Let go," she said. He loosened his grip, and she pulled her arm away.

"I'm sorry. It's a reflex."

"Why do you still have this?" She held the lock picking set up in front of him.

He snatched it out of her hand before she could pull it back. "Because I don't have a key to your house yet. The door was locked, and you didn't answer when I knocked."

"I'll get a key made for you today. Then, you won't need that anymore, will you?"

He took a deep breath. "I know I promised to be honest with you, but there are some things that you shouldn't know. It's for your own protection."

"I appreciate your concern for keeping me separate from that part of your life, but I worry about you. I'm so afraid that one day I'll get a call saying you've been arrested or something worse."

He took her into his arms and hugged her tightly. She liked the safe feeling she got whenever he held her in his arms. Nothing could hurt them when they were as one.

"I promise nothing will happen. You don't have to worry."

"How can you be so sure?"

A wry smile appeared on his face. "Because I'm good."

That made her laugh.

"Go get dressed and I'll take you to town to get your new phone."

She quickly dressed and came back out. As they walked through the kitchen to leave, she saw the daily newspaper on the table. Silas must have brought it in with him. "Wait. Mae stopped by earlier and said there was an article in the paper about the fire."

She grabbed the newspaper and sat down at the table to read it. A few minutes into the article and she folded the paper up and tossed it back on the table. "Have you read this?"

"No, but Austin told me about it."

"It says you're the prime suspect, even though you claim to have an alibi."

"It's garbage. Don't believe it. Everything will be fine once they speak with Mac."

"Yesterday, you didn't seem so sure."

"Don't worry. Let's go."

Keely sat outside the door waiting for them. "Hi ya, girl." Tessa leaned down and petted the dog. "Can she come with us?"

"Sure." They walked out to Silas' truck, and Tessa let Keely in first. She hopped into the backseat, taking her spot in the middle. Tessa climbed in and buckled up while Silas did the same.

Their first stop was at the phone store to get both of them new phones, and taking time to have lunch next. Finally, they drove to the hardware store to get a couple house keys made. When they got back to her cabin, a sheriff's car waited in the driveway.

"Silas." She looked over at him fearful of what they were doing there.

"It's okay. He's probably here to ask you about the fire."

Silas parked next to the police car, and they got out with the dog following.

"Mr. Newberry."

"Deputy Whitman. This is Tessa Cooper."

"Hello, Miss Cooper. I'm Deputy Steve Whitman, and I'm here to ask you a few questions about the fire that occurred at Mr. Newberry's residence."

"Certainly. Please come inside." She unlocked the door, and they all went in.

The deputy turned and stood in front of Silas at the door. "Mr. Newberry, I need to question her alone, if you don't mind."

Silas paused for a few seconds. "I understand. Tessa, I'll be back in about an hour. Keely, come."

Silas and the dog left and the deputy watched out the window until he drove off and then turned back to Tessa.

"I won't take much of your time."

She smiled at him, feeling both a bit nervous and anxious. "Please sit down. Can I get you something to drink?"

"No, thank you. How are you feeling? I understand you suffered smoke inhalation," he said, sitting down and taking out his notepad.

Tessa sat too. "I'm fine, thanks to Silas getting me out of the house when he did."

"You were very lucky." He paused before asking his next question. "Are you aware of Mr. Newberry's criminal record?"

"Yes."

"That doesn't bother you?"

"Of course, it bothers me. However, he's served his time and is working a legitimate job as a carpenter now."

"You don't think he's still involved in some illegal activities?"

"What does that have to do with the fire?" she asked.

The deputy didn't answer, but instead moved on. "Mr. Newberry said he received a call from a friend that needed his help, and then he left the house. Do you remember that call?"

"Yes. The ringing woke me up."

"Do you know what time that was?"

"It was around two when I looked at the clock. I went right back to sleep when he left."

He jotted down some notes. "Did he leave right away?"

"I think so."

"You don't know?"

"Like I said, I went back to sleep."

"Do you remember hearing anything, any noises?"

"No. You think Silas started the fire, don't you?" she asked.

"We don't know who started it yet. We have to check out all

possibilities."

"That's not what the newspaper article said. It said he's the prime suspect. Deputy Whitman, Silas didn't do it. He didn't burn down his own home, and he certainly wouldn't do anything to harm me."

The deputy wrote down a few more things, closed his notebook, and stoically said, "I think that's all the questions I have for now. Thank you, Miss Cooper." He got up and left.

Tessa was worried that she hadn't help Silas' situation with her answers. She paced around the kitchen trying to figure out what she could have said differently that would have helped more.

Hearing a car door shut outside, she looked out the window and saw Silas and Keely heading toward the house.

"How'd it go?" he asked after he walked in.

"I don't know. I answered all of his questions, but I don't know if he believed me."

"You told the truth, right?"

"Of course."

"That's all you needed to do." Silas got a bottle of water out of the refrigerator and sat down at the table.

A knock at the door interrupted them. Tessa answered it, and Martin and Elaine Pratt came in.

"We saw the police car over here and waited until it left before coming over," Elaine said. "We wanted to stop by and see how you were doing."

"I'm doing very well. Thank you. Would you like to sit down?"

The Pratts sat at the table with Silas, but Tessa continued to stand.

"If there's anything you need, Tessa, just let me know," Martin said.

"Why would you want to do anything for me?" she asked.

"Well, we're neighbors and neighbors help each other."

"Or, is it that you feel responsible for what happened since that Mac guy who works for you is the one that started the fire?"

"Tessa!" Silas shouted. "That's uncalled for. I'm sorry, Martin."

"Don't apologize, son. I assumed by now that she knew all about our connection to each other. You need to let her get it off her chest."

"You knew all about his record. Why would you put him in jeopardy by having him continue poaching those animals? Why would you even do it at all?" She was furious, and she couldn't hold any of it back now.

"It's simple. I do it for the money," Martin calmly said.

"Silas told me you were mad about those women at the bar. Maybe you started the fire to get back at him," she said.

"You're wrong about that."

"Enough," Silas said.

Tessa ignored him and continued on Martin, taking a step toward the table. "What if I told the police about your little business? What then?"

"Tessa, no," Silas said, taking a hold of her arm.

"That would be a very big mistake, little lady. If you did that, I'd hate to see what would really happen to your boyfriend."

Silas looked at Martin. Then at Tessa, who was looking at him.

She looked back to Martin and Elaine. "I think you should leave."

Martin shook his head and got up. "Silas, stop by and see me at the barn tomorrow morning."

"I'll be there."

Martin walked out of the house, but before Elaine left, she turned to Tessa. "If you ever want to talk, please stop by. It's not as horrible as you think."

Tessa could only stare at Elaine as she walked out the door. She stepped away from Silas. "They make me so mad."

"Why on earth would you threaten Martin like that?" Silas asked.

"I'm sorry, but I couldn't stop myself. Maybe I should go apologize."

"No, you've said enough. The damage is done. You let him know you know about his operation. You just got yourself involved in something very dangerous."

"I—I didn't realize. What should I do?"

"I really hate to say this, but I think you should move back north."

"You want me to leave?"

"I don't want you to go anywhere, but you're not safe here anymore."

She started pacing again. "I'm not leaving."

Silas could only shake his head. "I have to go out for a little while."

She stopped pacing. "Now? Where are you going?"

"I have a few things to do. I won't be gone long."

"You promised you'd always tell me where you were going."

"Darlin', after what you just did, all bets are off now." He opened the door and left.

* * * * *

CHAPTER 8

MORNING came too soon for Silas.

He rolled over and caught himself, before falling off of Tessa's couch where he slept last night. He had become so angry when he heard Tessa admit to Martin that she knew about his operation, he had to leave. When he returned later in the night, he didn't dare go into her room for fear of a big fight. She had no idea what she'd done. He sat up on the couch and rubbed the growth of stubble on this face. Standing up, he grabbed his aching back. It wasn't the worst place he'd ever slept, but Tessa's bed would have been better.

He went to the kitchen and started a pot of coffee and, after letting Keely outside, started frying some bacon for breakfast.

Tessa walked around the corner, entering the kitchen. "Good morning," she muttered.

"Good morning." Clothed in her pink terrycloth robe, fuzzy slippers, and hair pointing in all directions, she dragged herself over to the coffee pot. Even fresh out of bed, he thought she looked beautiful. "Would you like some breakfast?"

"Yes, please." She poured her coffee and sat down at the table. "Where did you go last night?"

Silas thought about how to answer her question. "I met Austin for a few drinks."

"Oh." She took a drink of her coffee. "You slept on the couch."

"Yeah."

"Why?"

"I didn't want to wake you when I got in, and I didn't think you'd want me in bed with you." He put the slices of bacon on two plates and cracked the eggs into the skillet.

"Did I say something that made you think that?"

"Not really. I just assumed."

"If I didn't want you in my bed, I would have told you." She took another sip of coffee. "What are you doing today?" Keely scratched at the door, and Tessa let her back in.

"I have to go see Martin today, remember?" Silas put some dog food in a bowl for Keely.

"Oh, that's right. He said something last night about the barn. What is that? He doesn't have a barn over there."

He put the eggs on the plates and brought them to the table. Silas sat down and debated about how much he should tell her. She already knew too much about Martin's operation and more would probably just make it worse. "It's just a place for us to meet."

"Where is it?" She took a bite of bacon.

"I can't tell you," he said with a mouth full of food and swallowed. "Like I said last night, it's for your own protection that you shouldn't know."

She pouted.

"That's not going to work on me. Not now. I'm not going to feel sorry for you and tell you things you shouldn't know. I will tell you I have a carpentry job to do this afternoon, so I'll be late getting here tonight." He continued eating.

"Can you tell me about that job, or is that a secret too?"

He knew she was teasing. At least, he hoped so. "I'm helping a guy hang some new cabinets in his home."

"What about that job you said you was going to get so you could get away from Martin?"

"It's still in the works, but there's nothing new on it."

"You're still not going to tell me about it, right?"

"That's right." He got up and took his empty plate to the sink.

"Just leave that over there, and I'll do the dishes later," she said.

He took the lid off of his travel mug on the counter, filled it with coffee, and then replaced the lid. "I can't take Keely with me today. I hope you don't mind if I leave her here with you."

"Not at all. She'll be good company for me. Make sure you take your jacket. It's supposed to get colder today."

It had been a long time since anyone cared enough to worry about him staying warm. He put his coat and knit hat on, and Tessa followed him to the door. He turned and gave her a big hug.

"What's that for?"

"I don't know, because you give a damn about me."

"Yes, I do. Probably more than you realize."

That's what he was afraid of, her caring too much and getting herself into more trouble because of it. "One more thing, don't let Martin or Elaine in the house. I don't trust either one of them."

"You don't think they would hurt me?"

"No, but they might try to do something to gain some control over you or implicate you in something. Just don't let them in, okay?"

"I won't."

Silas leaned down and kissed her. "I'll see you tonight."

"Be careful."

He looked back at her beautiful brown eyes. "I will." He stepped out the door and listened until he heard her lock it behind him. As he drove out of the driveway, he noticed Martin's truck wasn't at his house. No doubt he was already at the barn waiting.

When Silas reached the barn, he was right. Martin's truck was parked by the main door and was the only vehicle there. Silas went inside.

No one was around, but he saw a light coming from Martin's office. This wasn't going to be pleasant. He took a deep breath and walked in.

"Sit down," Martin ordered.

He sat in the chair in front of the desk.

"Tessa is quite a girl, isn't she? She really has a mind of her own."

"Yeah, she does."

"You know that's not a good thing, don't you?"

Silas shifted in his chair. "I know."

"What are you going to do about it?"

"We've had a talk, and she's going to stay out of that part of my life."

"Do you think she'll do that?"

He really didn't, but he wasn't going to admit that to Martin. "I trust her."

"You better hope she minds her own business, because if she doesn't, I'll have to take matters into my own hands."

"Martin, I like working for you. It's good money, but if you touch a hair on her head you'll have to deal with me."

"Well, let's both hope it doesn't come to that. Now, let's get on to business. I have another group of hunters coming in at the end of the week. I need you to take them out and before you ask, they're men."

"What are they hunting?"

"Bear. As an added bonus, I'm going to pay you a thousand dollars for each one they get."

"They must be paying you well for this trip."

"They are. You think you can accommodate them?"

"I think they'll have a better chance if I can get some bait out right away."

"Take Austin and do that. Oh, and Mac is at the police department as we speak, telling them that he called you the night of the fire."

"I still think he started the fire and if I ever find proof, I will kill him."

Silas got up and walked out.

* * *

LATE that same afternoon, Silas sat in his truck in the parking lot of the outdoor store where Austin worked waiting for him to get off work. Finally, he came out and walked over to the truck. Silas lowered the window.

"Hey, Silas. What are you doing here?" Austin asked.

"I've got a bear hunt in a couple days and need to get some bait out. Want to help?"

"Sure. I just got off work. Are you going now?"

"Yeah, I don't want to waste any time."

Austin got in the truck with Silas, and they headed out of town.

"You aren't going to believe this, but Martin is going to pay me a thousand dollars for every bear these hunters take."

"That's some serious cash."

"I'm hoping this will be my last job with him. I might just be ready to cash in and get the hell out of Dodge," Silas said.

"If you pull out of here, what about Tessa?"

"That's going to be complicated. When we first got involved, I thought it would only be for a year, but things progressed more than I thought they would. I'm not sure what to do. She has her old life and job up north. I don't know if I can ask her to change that for me."

"You're going to have to decide soon."

"I know. I need to figure out what's best for her."

They reached the area where they needed to lay the bait. Silas and Austin unloaded two twenty-five gallon barrels from the back of the truck. One had chocolate waste products in it and the other held liquefied peanut butter. Both men began emptying the barrels on the ground.

"Peanut butter and chocolate, two of my favorite flavors," Silas declared.

"Yeah, and the bears favorite too," Austin added.

It was near sunset when they finished. "Did you hear that?" Silas whispered.

"What?"

"A turkey."

In the near distance, the familiar gobble of a turkey could be heard. Silas slowly went back to his truck and got out his shotgun.

"What are you doing?"

"I want to get a turkey for Thanksgiving," he whispered.

The two men stood like statues next to the truck until they saw a tom turkey strut out from the trees. Silas took aim with his gun and fired. His aim was spot on, and the turkey dropped in his tracks.

"Nice shot."

"Thanks."

Silas retrieved the turkey and tossed it in the back of his truck. The men loaded the barrels back onto the bed and headed out. After dropping Austin off at his truck and unloading the barrels back at the barn, Silas went home to Tessa.

When he arrived, she met him at the door. "I've got a surprise for you," he said holding up the turkey by its feet.

She looked at him with wide eyes and ran from the door to the living room.

He laid the turkey down on the ground and ran in the house after her. "Tessa, what's wrong."

"You promised me that you wouldn't do any of your illegal stuff around me. Then, you bring home one of your poached animals!"

"No. You have it all wrong. This is a legal kill. It's turkey season."

"It's legal?"

"Yes. I told you things were going to change soon. This is just the beginning."

She gave a skeptical look.

"It's okay. I shot the turkey for our Thanksgiving dinner next month."

"Really? We're going to spend Thanksgiving together?"

"I hope so."

"I hadn't even thought about Thanksgiving."

"I need to go clean the turkey. I'll be back in the house in a little bit."

"I'll warm up dinner."

As an experienced hunter, it only took Silas a short amount of time to get the turkey plucked and cleaned. Afterward, he placed it in a garbage bag and put it in the large freezer in the house.

"Oh my gosh, you're a mess," Tessa said, looking at him. His clothes had blood and feathers all over them.

"Yeah, I need to go shower before supper."

"Would you like some help?" she teased.

"Why yes, yes I would."

After a long hot shower and then a romp in bed, they finally found their way back to the kitchen. "I think the food got cold again," she said.

"Isn't that what microwaves are for?"

"I believe so." She prepared a plate of food for each of them and warmed them in the microwave before they sat at the table to eat. "How was your day hanging those cabinets?"

"What? Oh, the cabinets. It went faster than we thought. That's how I had time to go hunting. This is really good food."

"Thanks."

After their meal, they retired to the living room to watch a little television and then back to bed.

The following afternoon, Silas was under his truck working on the engine with Tessa helping. At least, she tried. If she weren't helping, he was pretty sure he would have everything finished by now.

"Do you need another wrench?" She asked leaning over the engine and looking down at him.

"No."

While he continued to work under the truck, he saw two sets of legs approach. Mae Nicholson, along with a young man stopped as they walked by. "Hello, Tessa."

"Hi, Mae. How are you?"

"I'm fine. I wanted to stop and introduce you to my son, Chris. Chris, this is Tessa Cooper."

"Hello," he said, offering his hand.

Tessa shook hands. "It's nice to meet you. Mae, I didn't know you had a son."

"He just got out of the Army and home from Afghanistan."

"Really? How long were you there?" Tessa asked.

"I was there for two of my six years as an Army Ranger."

"Oh my, a Ranger. That's impressive."

Silas heard enough and crawled out from under the truck to see this guy. "Hi, I'm Silas, Tessa's boyfriend." He wiped his hands on this shirt and held out his hand to Mae's son.

"Hello. I'm Chris." The two men shook hands and sized each other up at the same time. Chris stood about four inches over Silas and had blond hair and blue eyes.

"Chris, how long will you be visiting your mother?" Tessa asked.

"Right now, I just want to hang out at Mom's for a while, and then I'll start looking for a job somewhere."

"He can stay with me as long as he wants," Mae said. "Tessa moved here from Illinois to spend a year writing a book."

"Really? What kind of book?"

"It's a mystery that takes place here in the mountains," she answered.

"I love reading mysteries. How soon before it's published?"

"I don't even know if it will be. It's the first book I've written." She giggled.

Silas rolled his eyes. He didn't like how she was acting around Chris at all.

"I'd love to hear more about it sometime," Chris said.

"Maybe you and Mae could come for coffee some afternoon, and I could tell you about it.

She was positively gushing over this guy. Before Tessa could say anything else, Silas jumped in. "It was nice meeting you, Chris, but we need to get back to work here."

"What are you working on?" Chris looked down into the engine.

"Chris could probably fix it for you. He did all kinds of mechanical work before he went into the Army," Mae said.

"Thanks, but I think I can handle it."

"Okay, if you have any trouble, you know where to find me." Chris turned to Tessa. "It was a pleasure meeting you, Tessa. I hope we see each other again, and I really want to hear about your book."

"It was nice meeting you too."

Chris and Mae started walking back to their home.

Silas crawled back under the truck while mocking Chris. "It was a pleasure meeting you, Tessa."

"Did you say something?" Tessa asked.

"No."

Once he finished with the truck, he and Tessa went inside. While Silas cleaned up, Tessa stood outside the bathroom door and talked about Chris.

"I think it's really refreshing to find a man, like Chris, who likes to read, especially mysteries. You usually only see women buying mysteries."

"Un- uh."

"I'd love to hear more from him about Afghanistan. Don't you think that would be interesting to hear about?"

"Not really." Silas stepped out of the bathroom wearing nothing but a towel and walked to the bedroom. She followed Silas while she continued talking about Chris.

"Maybe we could ask him and Mae over for dinner one night soon. What do you think?" She sat on the bed while Silas dug out some clothes.

"Will you stop talking about him?" Silas demanded.

"Are you jealous?" Her eyes widened.

"No. Why would I be jealous of him?"

"Well, you should have seen the way the two of you were looking at each other when you shook his hand today. I thought for sure you both were going to whip 'em out to see whose was bigger," she teased.

"Don't be silly. Mine would have been," he said without missing a beat.

Tessa rolled her eyes. "You have nothing to worry about."

"I'm not worried. I just don't like you talking to strangers." He pulled a long-sleeved sweatshirt on over his head.

"He's not a stranger. He's Mae's son."

Silas put on a pair of jeans and walked out of the bedroom. Tessa was right on his heels.

"You are jealous. Wow, I can't remember the last time someone was jealous over me."

"I bet your husband was jealous all the time, but you just didn't know it. Men don't like to show that side, and I'm not jealous."

He opened the refrigerator door and pulled out a beer, but before he could open it, his cell phone rang. The caller ID showed it was Martin. "I need to take this outside." He stepped out the door.

"Hello."

"Silas, it's Martin. Those men that you're going to guide tomorrow are in town early and want to camp out there tonight so they'll be ready for the hunt tomorrow. I need for you to go out there now."

"Tonight?" He took a deep breath and let it out. "How soon?"

"Now, before it gets too dark. You need to get to the barn as soon as possible."

"All of my camping gear burned up in the fire."

"I'll have gear here for you. Now, get your ass over here."

"I'll be right there." He ended the call and went back inside.

Tessa was waiting.

"I have to go out tonight," he said.

"Where?"

"It's another job for Martin."

"How much longer are you going to be involved in this?'

"I told you not long." He put his wallet in his back pocket and his knit hat over his head.

"This has to stop now."

"Trust me, Tessa. Just trust me. I won't be back until sometime tomorrow."

She turned and marched out of the room.

Damn it. Why can't she just understand I know what I'm doing?

He put on his coat and left.

Silas made a quick stop at the barn to get the camping equipment he'd need and then drove to meet the men in a secluded area in the Pisgah

National Forest in North Carolina. By the time he made it to the hunting area, it was dark. He met the two men, which were a father and his older teenage son. After putting up his tent and having a beer with the men, they all turned in for the night.

The next morning, after breaking camp, Silas and the two hunters lay on the ground waiting for the bear to come to the bait. They could hear the grunting of one in the distance and were growing impatient.

"Why can't we just go to the bear?" the father asked.

"Because I don't want to have to try to explain to a Park Ranger how you got your guts ripped out by a bear and why you had a gun with you when it's not bear season," Silas replied.

"Dad, we better just wait here," his son said.

It took about thirty minutes, but the bear finally came out into the meadow ahead them. The older man took aim and just as he was about to pull the trigger, Silas sneezed. *Bang!* The shot missed, and the bear ran back into the trees.

"What the hell!"

"I'm so sorry. I couldn't help myself. It's an allergy."

"We've been out here since last night, and you didn't sneeze once. You didn't want me to shoot that bear, did you? I bet you really want it for yourself."

"Mr. Parker, I don't even have a gun with me. I've been baiting that bear all week. If I wanted it, don't you think I would have gotten it before now?"

"We'll just have to sit and wait for it to come back," Parker said.

"It's not going to be back. The shot spooked him, and he's probably a half mile away by now," Silas explained.

"What about another bear? Do you think another one will come around soon?" the son asked.

"No, the shot would have scared them all off. I'm really sorry. Missed shots are chances that all hunters take."

"Your boss is going to hear about this." The father stomped back to his truck with his son following.

"I figured as much," Silas said to himself, heading to his truck.

The men drove off, but before Silas left he pulled a notebook from under his seat and wrote something down.

Silas took his time returning to the barn. He knew what would be waiting for him when he got there. As he drove up, he saw Martin's truck and some other vehicles belonging to his other workers, but not the hunter's truck. He unloaded the camping gear and put everything on the ground. He'd take it in later.

Inside, Martin was again waiting for him. "In my office. Now!"

He followed Silas into the office and slammed the door behind him. "Do you know how much you cost me today? Thousands! Thousands of dollars! You used to be the best guide I had. I don't know what's gotten into you. No, wait. I do know. That bitch who lives across the street from me."

Silas tried to control himself. "It wasn't intentional. I'm sorry."

"You're sorry? You've been saying that a lot lately. Get out of my face and don't expect to get paid for this job today."

Silas walked out of the office and past the four men sitting at the table. Outside, he got into his truck and left.

* * * * *

CHAPTER 9

COLD weather hit hard Monday morning, welcoming in the month of November.

Peak fall leaf season had long past with most of the leaves now lying on the ground. Tessa wished she had hired someone to rake the yard, but since she didn't and Silas wasn't home, she stepped into the building Silas had constructed and brought out the rake. She walked to the front yard, but as she rounded the back corner of the house, she saw a police car in her driveway.

"Hello, Miss Cooper," the officer said.

"Officer Whitman, right?"

"Yes. Is Mr. Newberry here?"

"No, he isn't. Can I help you with something?"

"I suppose you could give him a message for me. After speaking with his friend, Mac Conrad, we've cleared him as a suspect in the arson of his home."

"I told you he didn't do it."

"Yes, ma'am, I know, but we had to eliminate all possibilities."

"Have you determined who did do it?"

"No, we haven't. I'm afraid it will probably turn into a cold case."

"Won't that keep his insurance company from paying the claim?"

"We'll prepare a statement for the insurance company stating we don't believe Mr. Newberry had anything to do with the fire. That should satisfy their requirement for processing the claim."

"Thank you. I'll let Silas know. I'm sure he'll appreciate hearing the news."

"Good day to you, ma'am." The officer tipped his hat, got back into the police car and left.

Tessa began raking the leaves and noticed that Chris was in his mother's yard doing the same thing. When he looked her way, she gave him a little wave, and he returned the gesture, but continued raking, as did she. With the sound of the raking leaves nearly deafening, she didn't hear Elaine Pratt approach.

"Tessa."

She jumped. "What! Oh, it's you Elaine. I didn't know you were around."

"I'm sorry. Can we talk?"

"That depends on what you want to say."

"I saw the police car over here. I hope you didn't take it upon yourself to tell them anything about Martin's operation."

"Someone should tell them, but no, I didn't say anything."

"I don't know how you found out about it. Maybe Silas told you in bed, but you need to remember one thing, if we're arrested, Silas will be too. Then, I'll tell them that you started helping with the accounting only a few weeks after you moved here."

"That's a lie! I've never done that."

"Believe me. I've already started falsifying the paperwork to make it look like you did. If we go down, I'm taking you with me." Elaine shook her finger at her.

Tessa, still holding the rake, took a step toward Elaine. "I'd like to see you try."

"Hi, Tessa. I thought maybe you could use some help with your leaves." Chris had walked over from his yard.

"Hi, Chris. Thanks. This is Elaine Pratt from across the street. Elaine, this is Chris Nicholson, Mae's son. He just got out the army where he was a ranger stationed in Afghanistan."

"I've heard a lot about you, Mrs. Pratt," Chris said.

She didn't even acknowledge him. "We'll talk again, Tessa."

"I'm looking forward to it."

Elaine left with Tessa watching her walk back to her house. Chris moved in front of Tessa, blocking her view.

"Let's go inside your house," Chris suggested. He took her by the elbow and walked with her to the house.

"Thanks for coming to help," she said.

"I could hear you arguing all the way over from Mom's yard. What's going on?"

"Sit down. I'll get us some tea and explain." Chris sat down, and Tessa got the drinks and joined him at the table.

"Mom told me about the Pratts and what they're doing. I take it Silas is also involved?"

"Yes, but he's trying to get out. He said he has another job lined up in a few months. I just wish he would get away from all of it now."

"Silas seems like a really good guy. I'm sure things will work out for him and you too."

"How could you know that Silas is a good guy? You only met him for a short time the other day."

"First impressions and all that, but my mom said he's a good guy."

"Really? I didn't think Mae liked Silas at all. She's always warning me about him."

"Mother's just looking out for your well-being. She likes you a lot and doesn't want to see you hurt. I think she knows deep down that Silas is a good person and will take care of you. It sounds like he's involved in some pretty bad stuff though, but as you said, he's working to get out of it and in the end, I think it'll be okay for both of you."

"Elaine threatened to claim I'm involved too if I tell the authorities what they're doing. She said she's already started to make it look like I've helped with the bookkeeping. I can't say anything to the police. If I did, Silas would be arrested too. What do I do?"

"Maybe you should start keeping your own records of what you have already seen and heard. I'm sure she won't do anything, but if she does, at least you'd have that."

"That's a good idea." Tessa looked out the window when she heard something. "Silas is home. Please don't tell him about Elaine."

"I won't."

Silas walked in the door and looked surprised when he saw Chris sitting at the table with Tessa. "What's going on?"

"Hi, Silas. It's good to see you again. I was just on my way out. Talk to you later, Tessa." Chris hurried past Silas and closed the door behind him.

Silas took off his coat and hung it on the hook by the door and turned to Tessa. "What was he doing here?"

"We were talking about books. He loves to read, remember?" She picked up Chris' tea glass and took it to the sink.

"I don't like you being around him." He opened the refrigerator and got a beer out.

"You're still jealous."

Silas sat his beer down hard on the counter and walked over next to Tessa. "Damn right, I'm jealous. He's blonde, has blue eyes, tanned skin, tall, and muscle bound. Isn't that what women swoon over?"

Tessa finished washing the glass, dried her hands, and turned to Silas. "You have nothing to worry about. I love running my fingers through your long brown hair, and I can't resist your rugged, slightly bristled face with your deep blue eyes." She touched his long hair and ran the back of her hand down his cheek ever so lightly. "As for tanned skin, well if you remember, when we first met in August, you had very tanned skin from working outside so much and then there are those muscles." She ran her hands down his upper arms. "Every time I see you in one of your shirts that hug your muscles tight, I want to rip that shirt off with my teeth." She placed her arms around his neck and kissed him. He drew her closer in a hug. She didn't know how she could be so lucky to find someone like Silas, someone she had grown to love so much.

When the kiss ended, she made her final claim, whispering, "Most importantly, I love you, and you love me. So, like I said, you have nothing to worry about."

In one swift motion, Silas picked her up and carried her to the bedroom. He gently put her on the bed and lay on his side next to her. "I'm sorry I was jealous over Chris. I've never felt about anyone like I feel about you." He leaned down and kissed her.

"You're forgiven. Just know that I love you and no one else."

He smiled, and took her into his arms for a hug. She cuddled up next to him, and before either of them realized it, they had fallen asleep.

Later that night, they sat on the couch enjoying some popcorn while watching a movie. "Oh, I can't believe I forgot to tell you. Deputy Whitman stopped by today and said you've been cleared as a suspect in the fire."

"I knew I was cleared."

"You knew and didn't think to tell me when you got home?" She threw a piece of popcorn at him. "How did you know?"

"Martin told me Mac talked to the police and told them he did call me out that night."

"I'm glad we at least don't have to worry about that anymore. The deputy said that they are classifying the case as unsolved because they don't have any other suspects."

"That's okay. I know who started it, and I'll take care of it myself."

"You still think Mac did it."

"I know Mac did it."

"Please don't do anything. Can't you just forget it?"

"When something that terrible nearly happened to the one I love, I hold a grudge."

"I wish you wouldn't. I'm so afraid you'll get hurt."

"You don't need to worry about me," he assured her.

"Stop that! You're not Superman, and you're not invincible."

"Don't worry."

"How can I not worry when you start talking about revenge?"

"I won't say anything more about it."

She laid her head against his shoulder, and they continued to watch the movie.

"How much longer are you going to work for Martin?"

"Not long, maybe one or two more jobs, and then it will be time to move on."

"Move on to what, that new job you won't talk about? Is it another illegal job?"

"I told you it was a normal, legitimate job."

"But, you won't tell me what it is."

"It's a surprise. Now, watch the movie."

"Actually, I'm kind of tired. I think I'm going to go to bed." She got up and went to bed leaving Silas on the couch.

* * *

SILAS got up early the next morning leaving Tessa in bed and drove toward town. He had a long day ahead of him. Martin wanted him to build a storage room along one of the walls inside the barn, and he wanted to get an early start on it.

The barn was vacant when he arrived, so he unlocked the door, went inside, and turned on the lights. Even with its solid construction and insulation, it was still cold in there. He started a pot of coffee and then walked to the rear of the building where the lumber was stacked. He paused when he got to Martin's office and stared at the door. He'd love to get into that office and see what kind of records Martin had stashed in there. His lock-picking kit was still in his truck, but sure as he would get into the office, someone would walk in and catch him. Another time, maybe.

By the time some of Martin's other men arrived, Silas already had two walls constructed in the back corner of the building and was putting paneling up with a nail gun.

Mac and Greg appeared in the doorway of the new room. "Well, well, looky who came in early to get Daddy's praise for working so hard," Mac said.

"You should try working hard, Mac. You'd be surprised at how good it feels to work up a sweat doing a job you're proud of," Silas said.

"Yeah, I bet you'll have that bitch of yours soap you up real good in the shower once you get home," Mac said, laughing.

"Why don't you two go make yourself useful, somewhere else?"

"Tell me, Silas. What's that skinny bitch like in the sack? I bet she can just fuck the hell out of you," Mac taunted.

Silas was putting up a piece of paneling next to the door and quickly grabbed Mac, pulling him into the room. He slammed him up against the wall and held the nail gun against his head. "I'm getting a little tired of hearing your constant talking. I especially don't like you talking about Tessa." He slammed him against the wall again. "I know you started the fire at my place you son of a bitch, and when I find the proof, I will make sure I take care of you." He pulled him away from the wall and pushed him out the door.

Mac fell to the floor at Greg's feet and quickly got up. He looked back at Silas and pointed his finger at him. "One day soon, you and I are going to settle this once and for all."

"Just tell me when and where," Silas replied, taking a step toward him.

Mac didn't reply, and then he and Greg headed to the back of the building. Silas watched them until they were inside another room and then he went back to work.

Martin showed up at the barn an hour later and walked into the new room to check on Silas' progress. "This looks great. You do good work, Silas."

"Thanks. I ran the wiring in the walls before I put the paneling up, but I didn't connect it to the power. I'll leave that to someone who knows how to do the connections. That's not something I like to work with."

"That's fine. I've got someone who knows how to do the electrical connections." Martin walked around the room, inspecting the walls Silas had just put up. "Are you up for another hunting trip the coming weekend? I have a young man coming in that wants to shoot a turkey for his family's Thanksgiving dinner. Since turkey season's over, he needs to go somewhere he can be assured of getting a turkey and the authorities won't catch him."

"Sure, I can take him out. I'm surprised you want me out again so soon."

"Well, I'm sure that last incident wasn't intentional. Come to my office and I'll show you where I want you to take him."

The two men walked to the office, and Martin pointed to a spot on the map hanging on the wall. "Here. This is where I think you should take him to hunt."

"That's Sunbird Mountain. You want me to take him all the way up there?"

"Yes."

"Well, you're right that the authorities won't catch us up there. No one ever goes up that narrow road."

"There's a meadow about a half mile off the road here." He pointed on the map again. "That should be a good spot."

"Do you want me to go put some corn out this week to bait them in?"

"That won't be necessary. There should be plenty of game up there since no one hunts in that area. He wants to start early Saturday morning, so he'll meet you up there around six."

"I'll be there."

"Son, I don't have to tell you that this is your last chance with me. You screw this one up and you're going to be out on your ass."

"I understand. There won't be a problem."

Martin slapped him on the back, and Silas walked out of the office. He decided to take a break before going back to work on the storage room and stepped outside. The sunlight nearly blinded him, but it felt good on his face. He pulled out his cell phone and called Tessa.

"Hello."

"Hi, beautiful."

She laughed. "Silas, what do you want?"

"You were sleeping so peacefully when I left this morning, and I miss you. Can't a guy call his lady for a little pick-me-up?"

"Of course, you can."

"Are you working on your book today?"

"Yes, but its slow going. My mind is wandering."

"Well, you'll have plenty of time to work on it by yourself. I'm going to be late tonight."

"Why?"

"I thought I'd take Austin out for some beers tonight. It's been a while since we hung out together."

"I'll put a plate of food in the refrigerator for you in case you're hungry when you get in. Be careful."

"Thanks, I will. Bye."

"Bye."

Silas went back inside and worked some more on the storage room until he finished it late that afternoon. He walked through the building and found it to be a very busy place that time of the day. Several more men had shown up during, and they were working in the butcher room, processing several game animals that had been brought in the night before. He knew he had a job to do, but seeing this made him feel sick.

Tessa coming into his life had changed it all. He looked forward to the day when he didn't have to worry about looking over his shoulder to see if anyone were coming after him. He walked out the door and climbed into his truck to go meet Austin.

He pulled into the parking lot of the Eagles Nest Sports Bar and spotted Austin's truck already there. He walked inside and found him sitting at the bar and took the stool next to him. "How's it going?"

"It was a long day working at the store today. A lot of customers came in to do early Christmas shopping," Austin said.

Silas ordered a beer from the bartender and started nibbling from the bowl of pretzels in front of him. "Martin's sending me on another hunt this weekend."

"I'm kind of surprised. I didn't think he'd send you out on any more hunts. What's this one?"

The bartender sat Silas' beer in front of him, and the two men moved to a table. "Some guy wants to shoot a turkey for Thanksgiving, so Martin's sending us up to Sunbird Mountain," Silas said.

"That's kind of out of the way."

"I thought so too. Martin says the guy doesn't want to take any chances on getting caught."

"Yeah, no chance on that up there."

"I think this is going to be my last hunt and then I'll be ready to quit."

"Does Tessa have anything to do with that decision?"

"Some, but its time for me to get out of this. Sooner or later, my luck's going to run out."

"What's it like to come home to a beautiful woman every night?"

Silas smiled. "Until I moved in with her, I'd never even thought about something like that. Now, in the short amount of time I've been there, I can't imagine not coming home to her."

"What about when she's ready to move back north? What happens then?"

Silas took a drink of his beer. "I try not to think about that."

"It will be hard on both of you when she leaves."

"If she leaves."

"You think she won't move back north?"

"She really likes it here, so maybe."

"When this thing with Martin ends, won't you go back to Virginia?"

"Yeah, well maybe she'll come with me."

"You're taking a lot for granted, buddy."

"I'm going to take advice from a perpetual bachelor? I don't think so." Silas slapped Austin on the shoulder and laughed.

"Tessa's not mad that you're out drinking tonight?" Austin asked.

"I called her today and told her I was meeting you here tonight, and she didn't seem to mind."

Austin laughed. "Don't get too used to that. I've heard that doesn't last forever."

The two men ordered some food and after eating and then drinking a few more beers, Silas checked his watch and called it a night. "I need to get going. You heading home soon?"

"Actually, there's a girl over there that's been smiling at me all night. I think I'll go talk to her for a while."

Silas laughed and put some money on the table before saying goodbye. On the drive back to Tessa's, he did a lot of thinking about what Austin said. He hadn't told Tessa his next job would be in Virginia. He really hadn't given much thought to their future because he was concentrating on the present. What an idiot he was.

Silas found Tessa on the couch reading a book when he walked in. "I thought you'd be asleep by now."

"I was waiting up for you. Did you have a good time with Austin?"

"I did, but I'm really tired and want to go to sleep."

She walked with him to the bedroom and climbed in bed while he went into the bathroom. A few minutes later, he walked into the dark bedroom and climbed in bed. She snuggled up next to him.

"This feels really nice," he said.

"I know."

"I have another hunt to go on this weekend, and before you say anything, it looks like it will be my last job for Martin."

"You're finally going to quit?"

"I am."

She gave him a hug. "I'm so glad."

"We need to talk about something though." He struggled to find the words. "This—well, this new job that I'll be taking is in Virginia, so I'll be leaving here."

"Oh, I see. How soon?"

"I'm not sure. I'm still waiting for the final word on it."

She was very quiet and he wasn't sure what to say to her. He wished he could see her face in the dark. "Tessa, do you want to talk about this?"

"No, not tonight. I just want to go to sleep now."

"I don't like going to sleep when something's wrong between us."

"There's nothing wrong between us, I just really need to think about what you've told me. It's a lot to absorb right now."

"I don't understand. You always said you were going to go back to Illinois when you were finished with your book, but now that I tell you I'm going somewhere else, you need to think about it?"

"Silas, I don't want to talk about it now. In bed is not the time or place."

"I suppose you're right. I should have waited until tomorrow to tell you. Goodnight." He rolled over away from her, and she did the same from him.

* * * * *

CHAPTER 10

TESSA had a restless night of tossing and turning after Silas told her he would be moving back to Virginia. Getting up before dawn, leaving him alone in bed, she went to the kitchen and started the coffee.

She had hurt him by not wanting to talk about it last night, but he sprung it on her so unexpectedly. It was a touchy subject, and she didn't want to say the wrong thing without thinking it through.

She was in deep thought when Silas walked into the kitchen and startled her. "Good morning."

His disheveled look almost made her laugh with hair pointing in all directions, more of a beard on his face than usual, and those plaid pajama pants he wore were hideous.

"Good morning. I think the coffee's done, if you want some," she said.

"Thanks." He got a cup from the cabinet and filled it. "Would you like some?"

"Yes, please."

He handed her the one he'd just poured and got another for himself. "I'm surprised to see you up so early." He sat at the table with her.

"I didn't sleep very well last night."

"Yeah, me either."

"Do you want some breakfast?" she asked.

"No, thanks. I'm not really hungry."

They sat there in silence for a few minutes drinking their coffee.

"I'm sorry I didn't want to talk about Virginia last night. I wasn't expecting you to drop a bomb like that. I had no idea your new job would be somewhere else."

"I should have waited until today to tell you, and you were right, last night wasn't the right time to talk about it. How about now or do you want to wait?"

"It's as good of a time as any, I suppose," she said.

"I'll be moving back in my home town of Harrisonburg, Virginia."

"Have you known all along that you'd be moving?"

He took a drink of coffee. "Yes, for a while now. I need to ask you something."

"What?"

"When you first came here, you said it was for a year, and then you'd be moving back to Illinois. After all this time we've been together and confessed our love for each other, were you still planning on moving back there?"

"I...I don't know. I tried not to think about it. So much has changed since I got here and met you." He did it again, handing her the unexpected.

"As of right now, do you still plan on moving back to Illinois at the end of your twelve months?"

"I don't know." Tears swelled in her eyes. "Lately, I have been thinking of staying here and trying to find a teaching job at a nearby college. I really like living here. Then, you tell me that you're leaving and that sort of throws a wrench into my plan."

"What if I asked you to come with me? Maybe you could find a teaching job out there."

"You would really want me to come with you?"

"Until I met you, I've never even thought about sharing my life with someone. Now, you're all I think about all day or any time I'm not with you." He chuckled a little. "I've nearly run my truck off of the road a few times because I was daydreaming about you."

Tessa had a warm feeling throughout her body. "After my husband died, I didn't think I would ever love again. He'll always be special to me, but I've found that you've become just as special. I've never been to Virginia, but if it's as beautiful as Tennessee, I think I would love it."

"I know you would." He stood and pulled her up into his arms. "I can't think of anything any better than you coming with me."

After their decision had been made, Silas had to get ready for work. He took a quick shower, dressed, and came back into the kitchen. She had fried some bacon and made toast.

He poured some coffee into his travel mug, grabbed a handful of bacon, gave her a kiss, and was out the door.

"Be careful," she called after him.

After he left, Tessa got on her computer and did some research on Silas' hometown and thought it seemed like a pretty nice place to live. She couldn't wait any longer. No matter what time it was in Illinois, she picked up her phone and dialed Sara's number.

"Hello."

"Hi, Sara. I'm sorry to call so early, but I have some news for you."

"Tessa? What time is it? Is something wrong?"

"It's six o'clock and no, it's just the opposite. Silas is quitting his poaching job for a legitimate job."

"That's good, but couldn't that news have waited until I've had my first cup of coffee?"

"That's not all of the news. When he starts his new job, he will be moving to Virginia, and he's asked me to go with him." The phone went silent, and Tessa thought she might have lost the call. "Sara, are you still there?"

"Yes, I'm still here. I'm just a little shocked. Are you seriously considering this move?"

"I think I am. I've been reading online about his hometown, and it sounds really nice. There's a couple colleges close by where I might be able to get a job, and the countryside looks so beautiful."

"I don't know what to say. I may never see you again."

"Oh sure, you will. We'll keep in touch, and you can come visit. I'll come back there to visit too."

"Do you really love him enough to uproot your whole life?" Sara asked.

"You know, I think I do. I really do."

"Have you thought this through? What if you end up hating him once you're there?"

"I can't imagine ever hating Silas."

"If you're sure this is what you want, then I'll be happy for you."

"Thank you. Your blessing means so much to me. He doesn't know when his new job will start yet, so until he finds out, I guess we'll stay here, although I don't know why. If he's not working for the Pratts anymore, I'd rather we leave right away so they won't try to drag him back."

"That's a good idea. Do you think you can talk him into it?"

"I'll just have to see. Thanks so much for listening, Sara. I probably should go. Suddenly, I'm getting kind of sleepy and think I need to go back to bed for a while."

"Have a good sleep, Tessa. Bye."

Tessa ended the call. Even though she was excited about her new journey with Silas, the lack of sleep last night had caught up with her. All she wanted to do now was crawl back into bed. The only thing better would be if Silas were in there with her.

* * *

SILAS walked into the barn to work on a few guns Martin had asked him to do.

He probably knew more about repairing guns than any of them. It was something he had always known, but learned even more when he was in the Army. He went to the room where all the weapons were located and started working on the sights that needed to be tightened on several of the rifles. He also wanted to make sure his own guns were still there and in tip-top shape. There was no way was he going to leave them behind when he left.

While he was there, he heard the big garage door open up in the back and what sounded like a truck pulling in. Silas walked back to see what was going on. In the rear of the barn, a large box truck pulled inside and parked. The driver was talking to several of Martin's men.

"Hey, how you doing?" he said to the driver.

"Pretty good. We made a good trip last night. Take a look."

The driver took Silas around to the back where the other men were looking into the truck. Inside, he saw the bodies of several elk and bear.

"Let's get these unloaded," Martin called from behind them. The men climbed into the back of the truck and began taking out the animals and moving them into the butchering room.

"Silas, I need to talk to you," Martin said. They walked into the other room and sat at the table. "I'm willing to give you another chance with me. I've been doing a lot of thinking about this, and I think its time to have a second man in charge when I'm not available. I'd like that to be you."

He was a little confused since Martin had been so angry with him over the blotched hunting trips lately. "I thought you were mad at me. What's changed?"

"Think about the men that I have working for me. If I needed to put any of them in charge of something big, do you think they could handle it?"

"None that I can think of, except maybe Austin."

"Austin is good, but he's not been seasoned in this business like you have."

"Mac's not going to like me being put in charge."

"He'll get over it."

He had wanted to wait until this next hunting trip was over before he told Martin he was quitting, but now seemed to be the time. "Martin, I appreciate your confidence in me, but it's only fair to tell you after the hunting trip this weekend, I'm quitting and moving back to Virginia."

"What? Well, that's disappointing to hear, son. When were you planning on telling me, or were you just going to take off without a word?"

"I was going to tell you after I finished this weekend."

"Maybe you don't even want to do this last trip. You could just go now."

"If that's the way you want it, but I'd like to finish my last assignment for you. I'd like to leave in good standing."

"Say," Martin's eyes lit up, "you wouldn't be interested in branching out and doing this for me in Virginia, would you? I'd be very generous and offer you a fifty-fifty split. I'll even help you get everything set up out there."

"That's an interesting offer, but I'm getting out of this all together."

"Does Tessa have anything to do with this decision?"

"No, I made this decision without her. In fact, she got a little pissed at me when I told her I was moving back to Virginia."

"You probably made the right decision to get out of that relationship before she roped you in any tighter."

He wasn't about to tell Martin Tessa may be going with him. The less he knew about his plans, the better. "I better get back to work on those guns," Silas said.

He walked back to the armory area to go back to work, picking up a rifle to work on first. The barrel had just the start of rust forming on it. It frustrated Silas when people didn't take care of their weapons. He took a piece of fine steel wool, and began to gently rub it over the barrel to remove the rust, but not scratch into the metal. His thoughts drifted to Tessa and he questioned his relationship with her. Was it right to get her involved in his chosen life?

He finished with the rifle and began tightening the trigger of a handgun next. Tessa was an innocent bystander, and now was in the middle of something that could ruin their relationship.

Silas had just finished working on the last gun when Mac walked in. "Did you look at the sights on that 30-06 rifle of mine?"

"Yeah, I tweaked them a little. They weren't in too bad a shape."

"That's good because I have a real special prey I'm after. Martin told me that you're quitting."

"That's right, right after my last hunting trip this weekend." He kept polishing on a gun barrel.

"That's a shame. I bet that little lady of yours is sure going to miss you."

"I suppose."

"Once you're gone, she'll be fair game, so to speak. I might just have to go show her what a real man is like."

Silas picked up his handgun from the table, stood, and pointed it right at Mac. "A smarter man wouldn't have said anything like that about another man's girlfriend while that other man has an arsenal of guns in front of him. You really are stupid." He lowered his gun, placing it back on the table.

"You better keep an eye over your shoulder until you leave. You never know when you might get a surprise."

"You wouldn't shoot a man in the back, now would you, Mac?"

Mac just laughed and walked away.

Silas decided he had better leave before he and Mac had it out right there. He put on his shoulder holster and secured his gun. With his jacket on, no one could tell he was armed. He picked up both his rifle and shotgun and walked out of the room, past Martin, Mac, and Greg sitting at the table. "I cleaned all of the guns and fixed the sights on a couple of them. They should all be ready the next time they're used. I'm going to head out, if you don't need anything else."

"That should be all," Martin replied.

"I'm supposed to meet that guy up at Sunbird Mountain before dawn on Saturday morning, right?

"That's right. He knows the place. Now, you make sure he gets his turkey or his family is going to be mighty disappointed on Thanksgiving."

"I'll take care of it." Silas left the barn, anxious to get home to Tessa. He quickly headed to his truck and drove off.

He had an idea he was excited to ask Tessa about and hoped she would be just as excited. He drove up the road to her home, turned into the driveway, and jumped out running into the house.

"Tessa! Tessa, are you here?" Silas called for her when he walked into the house.

"I'm right here," she said, coming out of the laundry room. "What's going on?"

"What would you think of leaving for Virginia this weekend?"

A chill went up her spine. "You heard from that job?"

"Not exactly, but I know its mine, and I want to leave here as soon as we can after I finish this last job for Martin. We could spend Thanksgiving together in my hometown."

"Don't you need to get a place to live first?"

"I already have a place there. I'll need to get a small trailer so we can pull your car behind my truck. I don't want you to drive separate from me." He took her into his arms. "I want to see the look on your face when you see the mountains of Virginia for the first time."

"I don't think I've ever seen you so excited about something. Yes. Yes, if you want to leave this weekend, I don't see why we can't. I'll need to contact Mrs. Borden so she can tell the cabin owner that I won't be staying for the full twelve months, and I'll need extra boxes to pack the things I've added since I've been here."

"We can do all of that."

"I can't believe we're doing this," she said.

Silas pulled her closer for a kiss. He loved kissing her delicious, sweet lips. He reclaimed her mouth over and over again. He'd never met anyone like Tessa. Regardless of his history, she saw past that and only saw him for the good he had in him. No one had ever showed that much passion for him, and he loved her for it. He truly and deeply loved her.

He broke away from the kiss. "Tessa, I love you so much."

"I love you too, but I've got so much to do now. I have to get busy." She pulled out of his hug and sat down at the kitchen table. Grabbing a notepad, she started jotting down some notes.

Silas couldn't help, but laugh.

"Are you laughing at me?" she asked.

"Not in the way you think. I love how you can be a sexy, passionate woman one minute and turn into a take-charge woman in the next." He sat down with her. "I suppose I should take care of some things around town today too, so I can make a clean break. I'll be back before supper." He left the house and drove to Austin's apartment in town.

He knocked on the door, and Austin opened it for him to come in. "What are you doing here? Is something wrong?" Austin said, walking into the living room, followed by Silas.

"No, I just wanted to stop and give you some news."

"What's going on?" Austin sat down in the chair.

"I told Martin today that I'm quitting after the hunting trip this weekend." Silas took a seat on the couch.

"How'd he react to that?"

"He wasn't too happy, especially after he had just asked me to be his second in command."

"Seriously?"

"Yeah. Anyway, what I came here for is to tell you Tessa and I are leaving for Virginia this weekend."

"That soon and Tessa is going with you?"

"I know what you're thinking, but she and I have discussed this, and we both want each other in our lives."

"Well, I'm happy for you then." He reached over and shook Silas' hand.

"Thanks. Would you believe Martin wanted me to start a new branch of poachers for him in Virginia and was going to do a fifty-fifty split with me? I turned him down. I don't want to take any chance of him retaliating and doing something to Tessa. I want to get her away from here as soon as possible before anything happens. "

"You think he would do something like that?"

"I think he's capable of anything, and I'll be glad when you can get away from here too."

"That's the plan."

"Look, I need to get back to Tessa. I'll check back in before we leave."

The two men stood and shook hands again and then gave each other a quick hug.

* * *

WHILE Silas was visiting with Austin, Tessa walked up to Mae Nicholson's house and knocked on the door.

"Hello, pretty lady," Chris answered.

"Hi, is your mother home?"

"Yes, come in. Mom!"

"What is it? You don't need to yell. I'm not deaf. Oh, Tessa, I didn't know you were here, dear."

"Hi, Mae. I wanted to come and tell you the good news. Silas is quitting his job with Martin Pratt and moving to Virginia, and I'm going with him."

"What? You're moving to Virginia with him?"

She noticed Mae and Chris exchanging glances with each other. "Yes. We're leaving this weekend. Isn't that great?"

"What's he going to do in Virginia?" Chris asked.

"He hasn't actually told me yet, but he's promised that it's a regular job."

"Are you sure this is what you want to do? What about your teaching job in Illinois?" Mae asked.

"I still have several months to decide what I want to do, but if there's a college or university nearby, I thought I might try to get a teaching job there."

"It sounds like you have it all worked out," Chris said. "If you're happy, then that's what's important."

"I am happy, very happy."

"Congratulations, honey. I hope everything works out for you," Mae said.

Tessa saw Silas pull his truck into her driveway. "He just got home. I need to get back there. We have so much to do. I'll try to stop and see you again before we leave, but if not, thank you so much for be such a good friend to me." She gave Mae a hug and then left.

When Tessa reached the house, Silas was out in the backyard with Keely. "Where were you?" he asked when he saw her.

"I was at Mae's house. I wanted to say goodbye to her and Chris, in case I didn't get the chance before we left."

She walked up and gave him a kiss.

"What was that for?"

"For making me so happy. Oh, can you give me the address where we'll be living? I need to give the post office a forwarding address."

"Sure, I'll write it down when we go inside."

Keely came running back to Silas, and they all went into the house.

"Let's go out for dinner tonight?" Tessa suggested. "We need to celebrate our last few nights here."

"I suppose we could do that. I need to take a shower first though."

Three hours later, they sat at a table in the Black Bear Bar. Country music blared from the jukebox in the darkened room. A few people sat at the bar and about half of the tables were occupied. The waitress had already cleared their dishes, and they were enjoying their after-dinner drinks.

"I didn't think I'd be back in this place again after our last encounter here," Tessa said.

"I know. I guess it's only fitting that our last dinner in Yellowwood be here though." He reached over and took her hand. "Tessa, are you sure about moving to Virginia with me? I don't want you to feel pressured, if it's not what you really what."

"It is what I want."

"If you're sure. It's just that I've thought a long time about this move, and you've only considered it for a day. This is a big deal for you to pull up stakes and move somewhere you've never even seen before."

"Will you stop trying to talk me out of this? I'm very happy with my decision, and as long as I'm with you, I think I'd go just about anywhere."

"As long as you're sure."

"I am. Oh look, there's Austin." She waved at him, and he walked over.

"I thought you two were regular home bodies now. What are you doing out?"

"We decided to have one more night out on the town before we leave," she replied. "Would you like to sit down?"

"Thanks. I can only sit for a few minutes. I'm meeting someone."

"Anyone I might know?" Silas asked.

"Probably not. She's an auditor at one of the hotels down the street."

"Nice job getting a girl who gets discounted rooms for a quickie,"

Tessa teased.

Austin smiled. "It could come in handy. I suppose you're excited about going to Virginia?"

"I am, but I'm more excited about getting away from everything going on here. You should get out too, while you can, Austin," she suggested.

"I might just do that."

"That would be wonderful. I wouldn't have to worry about you then."

"You don't have to worry about me. Denise just walked in." He waved and stood to leave. "If I don't get to see you again, Tessa, take care of yourself." He leaned down and gave her a kiss on the cheek. "Take care of the old man here too." He patted Silas on the shoulder.

Silas stood up and shook hands with Austin. "Good luck with everything," Silas said.

"Keep in touch, buddy," Austin said and then joined his lady friend.

"Are you ready to go home?" Silas asked.

She just stared at him. "Do you realize what you just said?"

"I asked if you were ready to go home."

"That's the first time you've called my house home."

He threw some money on the table and held her chair as she stood. "Since you arrived, it's always been home to me," he whispered into her ear.

They walked out and got in his truck, but before driving all the way back to the house, Silas turned off of the main road and headed up a small lane.

"Where are we going?"

"Since we'll be leaving tomorrow, I wanted to show you a special place I like to go to sometimes."

Another turn onto a gravel road and a few yards later, it was as if the sky had opened up. He parked the truck and reached into the backseat for a blanket. "Come on, we can't see it from inside the truck."

They got out, and Silas brought the blanket to put around Tessa to help keep her warm. They walked to the back of his truck, and he lowered the tailgate to sit on.

"Just look up at that sky. Isn't it beautiful?" He put his arm around her.

Millions of stars twinkled throughout the whole sky. With no moon, it made it even easier to see them. "It is beautiful. Back home, there are too many streetlights. I've never seen so many stars."

Silas looked over at her, and when she looked at him, their lips met.

"Oh, look! There's a shooting star."

"Make a wish."

She closed her eyes tight and then opened them back up.

"What was your wish?"

"I can't tell you that."

Silas laughed. "Superstitious, eh?"

"You aren't supposed to tell your wishes."

"I'll tell you mine, because it's already come true." He leaned over and kissed her again.

She leaned her head against his shoulder. "I'm really glad you brought me here to see this. It's the perfect way to end my visit to Tennessee."

* * * * *

CHAPTER 11

VERY early Saturday morning, Silas got up and dressed for his last hunting trip.

He and Tessa had decided to not even wait until Sunday, but instead leave for Virginia today. After he finished with the hunt, he needed to pick up the trailer to haul Tessa's car and then get to the house so they can load his truck and leave. He was glad to almost have this part of his life behind him and move on to the next part with Tessa.

He let Keely outside for a few minutes while he got a bottle of water to take with him. He put on his sidearm, and his jacket over that, grabbed his phone, and was ready to go. Keely rushed back in when he opened the door and sat at his feet between him and the door.

"Get out of the way, Keely. I've got to go."

The dog stood up and moved closer to his feet and sat back down, whimpering. Silas leaned down and petted the dog. "You know something's up, don't you? Everything is going to be fine. Now, go to Tessa." With a wave of his arm, the dog took off to the bedroom.

Before going out the door, Silas looked around the room. He knew how the dog felt. He had an uneasy feeling too.

The sun had yet to rise, and with no moon out, it was pitch black as he drove up the steep, curvy dirt road to the top of Sunbird Mountain. When he reached the small dirt parking area, he saw an older model red pickup truck and a man getting out of it.

Silas stopped his truck and got out. "Are you Mr. Richards?" he called.

"Yes. Are you Silas?"

"I am." He walked over to the man, and they shook hands.

"You can call me John."

"It's nice to meet you. Martin tells me you want a turkey for Thanksgiving."

"I sure do."

"Well, if you're ready to go, we'll head up that trail for about a mile. It will open up to a field where there should be a flock coming along soon for their morning feeding. You can have your choice of the bunch."

"That sounds great. Let me get my gun."

The two men set off up the trail for the mile long trek.

"Why didn't you hunt for turkey during the season? It just ended about a week ago," Silas asked.

"I did, but never got one. If I don't get a turkey this time, I'm afraid we might not have one for Thanksgiving."

"Couldn't you just use the money you're paying Martin and buy one at the store?"

"I'm not paying Mr. Pratt for this. He was a friend of my late father, and he's doing this as a favor. I was laid off from my job about a month ago, and we really don't have the money for a turkey and the trimmings now. If I can just get me a turkey today, the rest won't matter."

It was the first time he had ever known Martin to do a good deed for someone. This man wasn't hunting illegally for the sport of it. He was doing it to feed his family. Silas wished he could help the man even more, but felt he wouldn't take any money from him. If he weren't leaving right away, he'd try to figure some other way to help. Maybe he could call Austin and see if he could have some food delivered anonymously to the family's home. Yeah, that's what he'd do.

By the time the sun came up an hour later, they were in place. Sure enough, just like Silas had said, right after sunrise they started hearing the familiar gobble of the turkeys, and not long after that, a few of them came out into the field below.

Richards took aim and shot. Down went the largest turkey in the bunch, and the others fled for their lives.

"Great shot," Silas said

"Thanks."

"Let's go get your turkey."

They walked down, and Richards picked it up. It was a big one. "If you wouldn't mind, would you take a picture of me with my turkey?" Richards asked.

"Sure. I'd be glad to. That is a great turkey. It should feed your family with lots of leftovers too."

Silas showed him how to position the bird for the photo and with Richards' cell phone he took the picture and then showed it to him.

"My family is going to love this."

"Would you like me to carry it back to the truck for you?" Silas asked.

"No, I'm doing it all." Richards picked the animal up by its legs with one hand and carried his gun in the other for the long hike back to their vehicles.

"I can haul it back to Martin's facility for you, if you want. I assume you're having him process it for you?"

"I am, but if you don't mind, I'd like to take it myself. I'm just not one for letting a stranger do things for me."

"I understand." He helped the hunter lift the bird into the bed of the truck.

"Let me get you a tarp to cover it. Since it's technically not turkey season, you don't want to drive through town with that bird visible in back of your truck."

"Oh, yeah. Thanks."

Silas got the tarp from his truck and covered the bird, securing it tight. "You go ahead to the barn, and I'll call Martin and tell him about your bird and that you're on the way in."

"Thank you, Silas." The two men shook hands. "I can't wait to tell my wife I got our Thanksgiving dinner now."

Richards got into his truck and drove off. This was the only time Silas felt really good about a poaching trip. He stepped up into his truck and dialed Martin on the phone.

"Hello."

"It's Silas. Mr. Richards got his turkey, and he's on his way in with it."

"Excellent. Are you coming here also?" Martin asked.

"Yes. I let him use my tarp to cover the bird, and I'm going to need that for my trip to Virginia."

"Good. I've got a little something extra for you since it's your last job."

"I'll be on my way soon." He ended the call and put the phone back in his pocket. He opened the glove compartment and took out that notebook, he started to write something in it, paused, then tossed it back inside without writing anything down, and closed the door. Starting his truck, he headed back down the mountain.

He hadn't gone far when he realized he was probably going a little too fast for this curvy road and applied the brake. The pedal went all the way to the floor, and he wasn't slowing down.

"Shit!" It was the worst feeling he'd ever had. No brakes.

With the steep grade, the truck kept accelerating at a fast pace. This little traveled road had no guardrails, and the curviest part was quickly approaching.

Silas gripped the steering wheel tightly and did his best to keep the truck on the road, but a hairpin turn was coming up. As he reached the turn, he tried to shift down a gear, but it was too late. He turned the steering wheel sharply and tried to maneuver away from the edge. His speed was too fast to control. The truck dropped off of the edge of the road and plunged down the mountainside, crashing into the trees below.

* * *

LATE that afternoon, Tessa kept herself busy by packing boxes. She'd been a little worried about Silas not showing up yet and had tried calling him several times with each call going to his voicemail. She figured he was held up trying to get that trailer thing to haul her car to Virginia.

When she heard a car door slam, she jumped up and ran to the door only to find a somber looking Austin standing there.

"Hi, Austin. Silas isn't here right now."

"I know. Can I come in?"

"Sure." She opened the door wider so he could step into the kitchen. "What's wrong?"

"Tessa, I need to tell you something."

"He didn't get arrested on his last hunting trip, did he?"

"Can we sit down?"

She could tell by his voice and the look in his eyes that something much worse had happened. "Austin, where's Silas?"

"There was an accident."

Upon hearing those words, she stopped breathing and felt a stabbing pain in her heart. She swallowed hard.

"Silas had an accident driving down the mountain, and he didn't make it. He's dead, Tessa. I'm so sorry."

"No...no...no! That's not true." Tears poured down her face. "Where is he? Where's Silas?"

Austin held her tight as she trembled from her sobbing. He took her to the living room where they sat on the couch, and she continued crying. Keely walked in and sat at her feet placing her head on Tessa knee.

Finally, Tessa looked up at Austin. "I want to see him."

"You can't."

"I want to see him, and I want to go now!" She stood up.

"Tessa, listen to me." He stood and held onto her shoulders. "His truck went off the side of the mountain and crashed a hundred yards down below. His body was so mangled you can barely tell it's him. You don't want that to be your last memory of him."

She laid her head against his shoulder. "They're sure it was him?"

"Yes. I identified his body." His voice cracked when he spoke. "I'm so sorry."

She sat back down on the couch. "What am I going to do without him?"

"I know you don't have many friends around here, but I'd be glad to stay here tonight, so you aren't alone. You really shouldn't be by yourself," he offered.

"No. I'll be okay. I'll call Mae up the road and tell her. She'll know what to do."

"Let me go up and tell her, and I'm sure she'll be right down."

"Thanks. I would appreciate that." Tessa stared out into mid-air, not really talking to Austin.

"Are you sure you'll be okay until I get back."

"I'll be fine."

"I'll be as quick as I can." Austin left her on the couch and went to Mae's house with the news. Keely stood and put her head on Tessa's lap again. "Oh, Keely, he's gone. What are we going to do?" When she said that, the dog actually whimpered a little.

A few minutes later, Austin, Mae, and Chris walked into the living room.

Mae sat down next her and gave her a hug, and Tessa broke down crying. "Bless your heart, honey. You go ahead and cry it all out."

"What am I going to do? First my husband and now Silas." She cried more.

"I'm sorry, Tessa. I know how much Silas meant to you," Chris said.

"Let me take you to the bedroom so you can lie down and rest," Mae said. "I'll stay with her tonight, boys. You might as well go on home. We're going to have some rough days ahead of us."

The two men left, and Mae took her to the bedroom. After a little sleep, Tessa was able to call Sara to tell her about the accident. Sara said she would be on the next flight down. Mae spent the night at Tessa's to make sure she was okay.

Sara arrived the next day, and Tessa sent Mae home, thanking her for taking care of her. Then, she and Sara sat at the kitchen table and talked.

"Did Silas have any family?" Sara asked.

"He said something about a brother named Kenny, who's in prison, but I have no idea where or how to get a hold of him. Maybe the sheriff would know how to get word to him."

"I bet he would," Sara said.

A knock at the door, it opened, and Austin walked in. "I hope I'm not interrupting."

"Not at all. Please come in and sit down with us." Sara said.

"Thanks. Hi, Sara." He sat down.

He looked at Tessa. "How are you feeling today?"

"Numb."

"That's understandable."

"Austin, you never told me why Silas' truck went off the road."

"I spoke with the sheriff this morning, and when they finally pulled his truck back up on the road and checked it, they found it didn't have any brake fluid in it."

"How can that be? He took better care of that truck than just about anything."

"I don't know. The sheriff said they couldn't find a leak in the brake line anywhere, so they're just as puzzled. Tessa, I also stopped by the funeral home today and spoke with the director there. He suggested, and I agreed, that you should make Silas' final arrangements."

She started to sob.

"I know it'll be hard, but I also know Silas would approve," he added.

"I don't know, Austin. That seems to be something that a relative should do."

"You're the closest thing he has to a next of kin. He would have wanted you to do this."

"Do you think, well do you think he would have wanted to be cremated? I think I'd like to scatter his ashes in the mountains. He loved the mountains so much," Tessa said.

"I think that would be perfect."

"Would you mind driving us down to the funeral home?" she asked.

"Of course, I will."

He took the two ladies to town to make the final arrangements for Silas. When they walked into the funeral home, Tessa waivered a little, and Austin caught her before her knees gave out. "Do you need to sit down?" he asked.

"I'll be fine."

An older gentlemen came rushing up. "Miss Cooper, I'm Thomas Quinn. I'm so sorry for you loss. Please come into my office and sit down. We can make the arrangements in there."

Tessa and Sarah sat in front of Mr. Quinn's desk. Austin stood in the rear of the room. "Ms. Cooper did you have any thoughts about Mr. Newberry's service?"

"I think he would like to be cremated and his ashes spread in the mountains."

"That sounds like a wonderful idea. Cremation will take a couple days, so we can set the service for Tuesday.

"That sounds fine." Tessa dapped her eyes with a tissue. "One more thing. Silas was a veteran. Could we have a flag displayed for him?"

"Yes, I'll see to it that a flag will be on a pole next to the ashes." Mr. Quinn jotted a few notes down on a pad of paper. "The last thing I need to know is about payment for the funeral."

"I'll take care of that," Austin said.

Tessa and Sarah turned around and looked at Austin.

"There's been donations made by several people around town, and it should be enough to take care of the funeral," he explained.

"Very well. That should take care of it. Again, Ms. Cooper, I'm so sorry for your loss and if there is anything else you need, don't hesitate to call me."

"Thank you."

Two days later, the funeral was held with only a handful of people attending. The Pratts were there, as well and Mae and Chris and, according to Austin, a few of the men attending were guys who worked for Martin and knew Silas. She did not see Mac Conrad in attendance.

After the service was over and the people had left, the funeral director gave Tessa Silas' ashes.

"Thank you." She turned to Austin. "Can we go do this now?"

"Of course."

Tessa asked Austin to take her and Sara to the place Silas had taken her to look at the stars, and he did just that.

They stood at the edge of the field. "Silas loved the mountains so much. I think it's only right this should be his final resting place." She opened the urn and let the ashes drift away with the wind. "I love you, Silas," she whispered, as tears rolled down her cheeks.

* * *

Two days later

"TESSA, look at this," Sara called to her. She came into the living room and showed Tessa a newspaper article about the arrest of an illegal poaching ring located in the mountains.

"Oh my gosh, let me see that." Tessa took the paper and began reading. "They arrested the Pratts and that Mac guy Silas didn't like. Thank goodness it doesn't mention Austin."

"It sounds like Silas was getting out just in time."

"I know. I'll have to call Austin later and see if he's seen this."

"Tessa, I hate to say this, but it's time for me leave to catch my flight back home. I hate to leave you here by yourself after all that's happened," Sara said.

"I'm fine, and you need to get back to work."

"Why don't you load all of these boxes into your car, and we can drive back home together. You shouldn't stay here by yourself."

"No, I have some things I still need to do down here. I'm actually thinking about going to visit Silas' hometown in Virginia, so I can see what it's like. Maybe even find someone there that knew him."

"Well, okay. I need to get going to the airport. Please take care of yourself." She and Tessa hugged for a long time before Sara went out the door. "Call me anytime you need to talk, okay?"

"I will. Thank you, Sara. I couldn't have gotten through this without you. I love you like a sister."

"Same here, girl." Sara got into the rental car and drove off.

Tessa sat alone again, but she had Keely to take care of now, who sat at her feet. She looked at all the boxes she had packed in anticipation of the move to Virginia, but didn't have the strength to unpack anything. She took Keely out to the backyard and sat in a chair while the dog made her usual rounds. Tessa looked over at the shed Silas built and remembered watching him work out there, hair flying in all directions as he put up the walls. How could she ever forget that sweet smile he had every time she took him something to drink. She caught herself smiling. She did have some wonderful memories of him that she'll cherish forever, and she had Keely. She would take good care of her because Silas would have wanted her to.

She pulled her cell phone out of her pocket and dialed Austin's number. It went straight to his voicemail. "Austin, I saw the newspaper today. Call me when you get a chance." She ended the call.

Around suppertime, Tessa actually started to feel a little hungry. With little food in the house, since they had planned on leaving, she decided to go to town and get a sandwich. She went to a drive-thru window for some fast food and then drove over to Austin's apartment. She went to his door and knocked, but there was no answer. While she was standing there a lady came out of another door.

"Are you looking for the guy that lived there?" the lady asked.

"Yes. Do you know where he is?"

"He moved out this morning."

"He did what?"

"Yeah, I saw a moving truck out in the parking lot, and he was loading it up. Seemed like he was in a real hurry too."

"Thank you." Puzzled, Tessa walked back to her car and left. He must have wanted to get out of town before he was arrested too, she thought.

Instead of stopping at her house, she drove past to Mae's house. She pulled into the driveway, got out and went to the door. Chris answered. "Hi, Tessa. Come in."

"Thanks, Chris. Is your mother home?"

"Yes, she'll be right out. How are you feeling today?"

"I'm a little better each day, I guess."

"Hello, Tessa dear. What are you doing here?" Mae asked, entering the room

"I was feeling a little low and thought I'd stop by for a few minutes."

"Is something wrong?"

"Actually, yes. I stopped to see Austin while I was in town a few minutes ago and he's gone. His neighbor said he moved out this morning."

"Where did he go?" Chris asked her.

"I don't know. He never said anything about leaving, but I was wondering if it might have something to do with that article in the newspaper today about the poaching ring. Did you see it? Austin was a part of that and, like Silas, was about to get out of it. I thought maybe he might have been arrested, but his name wasn't mentioned in the article, or maybe he was the one that turned them all in. I don't know."

"Could be either, honey. I wouldn't worry too much about Austin. He seemed like he could take care of himself just fine."

"I hope so."

"Would you like to stay for dinner, dear," Mae asked.

"No, but thank you. I picked up something in town. I should be going."

Chris walked Tessa to the door. "Try not to fret over Silas' death for too long. I doubt he would want you to."

"I know. Thanks, Chris." She stretched up, gave him a peck on the cheek, and then drove home.

Tessa slept better that night and when she awoke the next morning was surprised to see it was after nine-o'clock. She got up and didn't feel as tired as she had yesterday. She knew that grieving over Silas would eventually lessen. After all, she had gone through this when her husband died, but it was different this time. She had months to prepare for Colin's death and deal with the grief. With Silas' death, it was so unexpected.

She walked into the kitchen and opened the door to let Keely outside and then started the coffee. She sat at the table and looked around the kitchen. "Darn it, I still have Mae's containers that she brought me food in a few days ago. I'll have to take those back to her later."

She heard scratching at the door and let Keely back inside. She put some food out for the dog and then fixed herself a couple of pieces of toast. Her appetite still wasn't back to normal, but she knew she needed to eat something.

After taking a shower and applying a touch of makeup, she started to feel a little more normal. "Keely, stay here while I take these back to Mae." The dog sat down.

Tessa picked up the bowls, grabbed her car keys, and drove up to Mae's house.

She got out of the car and walked to the front door. After knocking and no one coming to the door, she walked to the main window and looked inside. She couldn't believe what she saw. The house was empty. No furniture and nothing on the walls.

She walked to the garage next to the house and tried opening that door, but found it locked. She went to the back of the house and looked in all the windows. Every room was stripped clean.

"What the hell is going on?"

She drove back at her house. "First Austin and now Mae and Chris. Why is everyone disappearing?"

Keely looked up at her and cocked her head to the side.

"I don't understand. If they were leaving, why didn't they say something yesterday when I was there? Oh Keely, you and I truly are alone now."

The next morning, Tessa heard a knock at her front door. When she opened it she found Deputy Whitman standing there. "Good morning, Miss Cooper. I'm sorry to bother you the day before Thanksgiving, but could I come in and speak with you?"

"Yes, of course. Come in." The deputy stepped inside, and Tessa closed the door. "Please, sit down. Can I get you something?"

"No, thank you." They both sat.

"You really aren't bothering me. I'm afraid Thanksgiving is going to be just Silas' dog and myself. I'm not really feeling much in the festive mood."

"I understand. I never had a chance to talk to you about Mr. Newberry's accident."

"Go on." She felt apprehensive waiting to hear what the deputy had to say. Keely sat at her feet, and she rubbed her head.

"I'm sure you've heard that no brake fluid was found in the reservoir or the lines of the truck."

"Yes, I did hear that. I also heard that the lines were fully intact with no leakage."

"We attributed the lack of brake fluid to poor maintenance, but after talking to a friend of Mr. Newberry's we understand just the opposite."

"That's right. He was very particular about his truck."

The deputy hesitated for a few seconds that felt like minutes to Tessa. "You've found something else, haven't you?"

"We have. We know that Mr. Newberry was involved with that poaching ring the Forest Service has made several arrests for. After some thorough questioning, it was discovered that Martin Pratt ordered one of his men to see to it that Mr. Newberry would be killed in an accident."

Tears swelled in her eyes, and she plucked a tissue from the box next to the couch to dab her eyes. "Who was the man that Martin ordered to do it?"

"Mac Conrad. I believe he was the one Mr. Newberry said called him for some help the night of the fire."

"Yes, that's right. I'm not surprised he was responsible for the accident. He hated Silas."

"Mr. Conrad has been arrested and charged with Mr. Newberry's murder."

"Thank you for the information, Deputy. I appreciate you letting me know."

"I am sorry for your loss, Miss Cooper. The accident was a real tragedy."

"Thank you." The deputy left and Tessa sat back down. "He was murdered." She began to cry.

* * *

The next day

THANKSGIVING was not a day Tessa had looked forward to, but it had arrived. She and Silas had planned on being in Virginia and having their first Thanksgiving together. Yesterday, she started thawing the turkey he killed last month for their dinner and decided to honor him by preparing the bird. It would be too much for her to eat alone, but she could freeze the majority of it to eat later.

She had just put the turkey in the oven when she heard a car door slam outside. "What the hell? Can I not get any privacy?" She looked out the window and saw a black sedan with a U.S. Government plate on it and a man limping to the kitchen door. Typical government man, she thought, wearing a suit and tie, plain overcoat, dark glasses, and short hair. She waited until he knocked and then opened the door.

"Tessa."

She stared at the man for a long time. Then, he took off his sunglasses.

She looked at his blue eyes. "Silas?" Her whole body quivered, but there was no mistaking those gorgeous eyes. "Oh my God, Silas!" She felt her knees give out, and he must have noticed too because he quickly jumped inside and caught her in his arms. She then gave him the biggest bear hug she could muster.

"Is it really you?"

"It's really me, but I can't be seen." He closed the door and took her back in his arms, kissing her long and hard and then he said, "I'm sorry."

Tears streamed down her face, but she wouldn't let go of him. "They said you were dead, killed in the accident."

With this thumb, he wiped the tears from her cheek. "Let's sit down on the couch and I'll explain everything."

They walked into the living room. Keely jumped up from her bed and ran to Silas, jumping up on him. He kneeled down to her, and she licked his face. "It's good to see you too, girl."

He sat on the couch with Tessa. "What is going on?" she asked.

"I've got so much to explain, and you have every right to be angry at me. When I'm finished, if you never want to see me again, I'll understand. I won't like it, but I'll understand."

"Please, just tell me."

He took a deep breath. "I've gone over in my mind so many times how I was going to tell you, and now I'm at a loss for words."

"Silas." She squeezed his hand.

"Okay. I guess the first thing I need to tell you is that my last name isn't Newberry. It's Conner. I'm not a carpenter, at least not by trade, or a poacher. I'm a law enforcement ranger with the U.S. Forest Service, and I've been working undercover for the past three years infiltrating the poaching ring. I'm sorry I misled you, but I was in so deep with my cover, I couldn't take the chance of anyone else knowing."

"So, the last four months between us have been a lie?" She let loose of his hand.

"No, not what was between us. I think I fell in love with you the first day we met, right out there in that driveway when I came to work, and I still love you."

"I'm so confused by all of this." She got up and walked around the room. "Your accident never happened?"

"Oh, it happened, and I was hurt pretty bad. I managed to jump out of the truck right as it went over the edge of the mountain. Luckily, I had my cell phone in my pocket and called Austin to come help me. I was in the hospital for about a week."

"Austin! He's the one that told me you were dead and said he identified your body."

"Austin's a Forest Service Ranger too and also working undercover."

"I tried to find him the other day, but he was gone."

"He was pulled out right before the arrests were made and so were Mae and Chris."

"Mae and Chris?" She sat back down on the couch. "My head's spinning. How could you go on those hunts helping people shoot the animals? Won't that cause you to get into trouble when all of this goes to trial?"

"I think that was the hardest thing about this assignment. Most of the time, we knew about all of the hunts enough ahead of time that we were able to find some old or injured animals for the poachers to shoot. I personally never shot or killed an animal illegally, and I was fortunate that the Forest Service was able to get my notebook out of the truck where I had recorded the names of all the hunters."

"This was really dangerous for you, wasn't it?"

"Remember when you asked me once why I carried a gun all the time? Now you know the real answer."

"Mae and Chris were in on this too?"

"Mae is actually my supervisor and Chris is another ranger, not really her son."

"Mae tried to talk me out of being in a relationship with you. I didn't think she even liked you."

Silas laughed. "Yeah, she wasn't one bit happy to find out how I felt about you, and she did try to split us up. If you remember, she's the one who suggested eating at the bar where you saw me with those women? She knew I was going to be there and set you up, hoping you would catch me with those women end the relationship. It almost worked too, but when she realized that wasn't going to happen, she gave her blessing and tried to keep tabs on you. After the fire at my house, we figured out it was Mac who started it."

"How did you know?"

"We found some candy wrappers along the edge of the woods. It was wrappers from the same candy Mac always ate and was always leaving those wrappers laying around. He had been out there watching the house when he called me, but he didn't know you were inside."

"The sheriff's deputy told me Mac confessed to starting the fire."

"Yes, he did, and after I started living here, we needed to keep you safe when I wasn't around, so we brought Chris in as Mae's son to watch the house when I wasn't here."

"You were so jealous of him."

"Yeah, I'm good undercover, aren't I?" He smiled and grabbed her hand, giving it a squeeze.

Tessa let her guard down and started to laugh.

"I still don't understand some things."

"What's that?"

"What about your criminal history that I found online?"

"Planted by the FBI for the Forest Service."

"You've never been arrested for anything?"

"Never. I'm a law enforcement ranger."

"You don't have a brother in prison in Virginia?"

He sucked air in through his teeth as if in pain. "Well, that one is sort of true and sort of not."

"I don't understand."

"My younger brother, Kenny is a Correctional Officer in Virginia. So, technically he is in prison almost every day."

"That is so not fair." She playfully punched him on the arm.

"Ow!" He rubbed his arm.

"I'm sorry. Did I hurt you?"

"I'm still a little sore from the accident. Any more questions?"

"Are you really from Virginia?"

"I am. Harrisonburg, Virginia is really my hometown. That's where I worked until I took this undercover assignment and the job I will be going back to."

"That's the job you were talking about taking in Virginia."

"I couldn't tell you what it was because it would have broke my cover. I'm so sorry, Tessa." He gave her hand another squeeze.

She pulled her hand away. "The day of your accident, we were going to leave that afternoon for Virginia. Just when were you planning on telling me the truth?"

Now it was Silas turn to get up and walk around the room. "I should have told you the day before."

"You should have told me a long time ago."

"I know, but I couldn't, and you have to know you were never in any danger."

"Except when your cabin was burning down," she reminded him.

"That was a major mistake we never saw coming."

"So again, when were you going to tell me the truth?"

"I was going to tell you several hours into our trip. I didn't want you staying here by yourself after they started arresting everyone in the ring. If they had missed someone, you would have been in danger. I had planned on telling you after I was sure we were far enough away from here that if you got so angry you changed your mind about coming with me, you would go back to Illinois, rather than back here."

"This is so much to absorb. You have no idea what I have been going through for the last few weeks thinking you were dead. Then, everyone just disappeared, first Austin, and then Mae and Chris. I had no one to lean on."

Silas kneeled in front of her and held her hands. "I knew what you were going through. Austin, Mae, and Chris kept me updated, and it was killing me. Tessa, I never wanted to hurt you, but the accident was the perfect scenario to fake my death. Martin needed to think I was dead, not just hurt, so they wouldn't try again."

"I spread what I thought were your ashes in the mountains. Whose ashes were they?"

They were just plain old wood ashes. The Forest Service had to bring the funeral director in on the fake death."

"I should be so angry with you, but all I can think about is how relieved I am that you're alive." She reached up to touch his hair. "What happened to your beautiful long hair?"

"The Attorney General that's handling the poaching case doesn't want anyone to know I'm alive until the trial. You have no idea how long it took me to talk their office into letting me come here today to see you. I had to cut my hair and put on this monkey suit to help disguise me. Believe me, once I'm back at my regular job, the hair will be grown back out."

She laughed and gently touched the side of his face.

He grabbed her hands again and held both of them. "Tessa, I love you with all my heart. Do you still love me enough to come to Virginia with me? We can start all over again, if you want. I'll even find you your own place to live until you decide if you want to be with me."

"I do still love you, Silas. I really do, and I don't want to live apart from you ever."

He smiled and kissed her. "The Justice Department has put me up in a nice hotel in Johnson City, and it has a very comfortable king size bed much too big for me to sleep in alone. Come back with me. Please."

"What about all of our things, and I just put your turkey in the oven for Thanksgiving dinner."

"The turkey I shot?"

"Yes."

He thought for a few seconds. "Let me make a few calls, and I'll stay here tonight. That is if you'll let me, and we can have the Thanksgiving dinner we planned. Tomorrow, we can travel to Johnson City and then on to Virginia. They'll send a moving truck for all of our things."

"Of course you can stay here."

He pulled her up into his arms and they hugged.

"Silas." She leaned back away from him. "It'll be a few hours before the turkey is done. How about I show you how happy I am to see that you're alive?" Tessa took his hand and led him down the hallway to her bedroom.

The End

About the Author

Carol Preflatish worked in social services for over thirty years. Her interest in writing began in high school as a reporter, photographer, and sport's editor for the school newspaper. Because of her interest in history, she co-authored "A Commemorative History of Crawford County, Indiana 1818-1993." One of Carol's favorite hobbies is photography. She has had many photos published in her local newspaper, as well as in the July 1997 issue of *Golf Journal*, the official publication of the United States Golf Association. Publications include several romantic suspense novels and two non-fiction books. Carol is a member of the Sisters in Crime organization. She lives in southern Indiana and shares a log cabin with her husband and two cats in what seems like an enchanted forest with a menagerie of wildlife constantly visiting.

* * * * *

www.ingramcontent.com/pod-product-compliance
Lightning Source LLC
Chambersburg PA
CBHW022020170828
46808CB00003B/999